I0566105

Lure of the Long-Legged Blonde

By
Norman Mark

BeachHouse Books
Chesterfield Missouri, USA

Copyright

Graphics Credits:

Cover by Dr. Bud Banis. based on a stock photograph from Arc Media Inc. with text and enhancements by Dr. Banis.

Publication date 2005

ISBN 1-888725-57-5 BeachHouse Books Edition an Imprint of

Library of Congress Cataloging-in-Publication Data
Mark, Norman.
  lure of the long- legged blonde / by Norman Mark.
    p. cm.
  ISBN 1-888725-57-5 (alk. paper)
  I. Title.
  PS3614.O7625L87 2005
   813'.6--dc22   2005031979

BeachHouse Books

Science & Humanities Press

PO Box 7151
Chesterfield, MO 63006
(636) 394-4950

Lure of the Long-Legged Blonde

Chapter One

I'm so tough Alka-Seltzer doesn't melt in my mouth. Call me your on-time, as-needed, quick-turnaround, zero-inventory gumshoe for today. When the going gets rough, I'm the go-to guy when everyone else has gone. If you understand any of that, you're better at this mumbo-jumbo than I am.

Example: the first 20 days of my intensive 24/7 surveillance of Merry Martha McConklin resulted in 480 snapshots of a beautiful woman turning over in bed in her flimsy nightgowns. Just doing my job.

I caught Merry Martha tossing and turning in pink and black baby dolls, in tap pants and scanty tops, in floor-length outfits that were slit up to there and beyond, and in green Peter Pan sleepwear complete with the little triangular hat favored by both Mary Martin and Robin Hood.

I had enough snapshots to populate a year's worth of Frederick's of Hollywood and Victoria's Secret catalogues. Unfortunately my client, Mortimer McConklin, wanted absolute proof of his wife's infidelities, and she was always alone when she slept. She was always alone.

That is, until on the 21st day, when she was with someone. While she was with him, he had wild passionate sex with her in four different positions with the help of Smucker's Blueberry Jam, a vibrator set at industrial speed and a slinky toy that ended with the mustached face of Kermit the Frog.

Unfortunately, on that vital 21st day I got no pictures I could share with the angry husband, my client. That was the day--actually the night--when Martha caught me in her bedroom, forced me to undress completely including the removal of my autographed Bud E. Love white cotton briefs, and humiliated me for three long hours. It was also the day we began our torrid, squishy and eventually squalid little affair.

I know, I know. Our passionate assignations probably violate the code of ethics of the professional detective. In my defense, as far as I am able to determine, detectives have no ethics whatsoever.

There is no detective's union to penalize private dicks that don't live up to whatever unenforceable code we might have. There is no entrance exam or licensing board administering the detecto-cratic oath, the way doctors have their group morality enforced by the Hippocratic oath, which I believe states among other things, "Thou shalt do enough tests on any patient to support all future payments on your sail boat."

In the past, detectives had morals to burn. The incomprehensible, supposedly "heroic" detective Philip Marlowe in Raymond Chandler's "The Big Sleep" refused a $1,500 bribe, offered to give back money if his client wasn't happy with the results, threw a gorgeous willing woman out of his bedroom and then ripped off the sheets even though they had only been used by the bedbugs.

I, on the other hand, would have taken the bribe, kept the client's money and gratefully boffed the blonde without thinking a second or even a first thought. For an additional $1.50, I'll work for your worst enemy, so you better keep me well paid.

Wait, I just remembered another person with no ethics-- the accountant for crimescene.com who refused to allow my penis extension as a business expense. Jerri Manning, a

2

small-minded, pinch-faced woman who devoted her life to narrowly defining every rule in the book, denied my claim even though I frequently employed my private member in constant efforts to get new clients, improve the bottom line and the public image of the company.

Jerri Manning, I hope that some day you are stuck on a deserted island for 15 years, that you are starved for sex, that I am washed on to that island and, after crying and pleading to use this dick's dick, I tell you in a most respectful way, "Sorry, but I cannot extend that for you."

Call me Sam Spade. Hell, call me Ishmael, if you want a fat lip. But be sure to call me in time for dinner, something my Uncle Guido always said.

Actually, my name is neither Sam nor Ishmael. Those were references I put into this narrative for dramatic effect to snooker you into the story. So let's start again.

My current name is Tony Testa. I should admit that I was born Antonio Primo Testosteroni (pronounced like macaroni: test-tost-er-ohn-neee). Then my dad legally shortened our family's last name after my Uncle Guido Testosteroni was frequently photographed entering squad cars with his hat covering his face. When the time is right, I'll tell you as much as I can about my Uncle Guido, my invaluable sidekick.

As for me, I never saw a law that didn't need a little breaking now and then. That is, except for the law which prevents sexual congress with she goats. I would never violate that law unless I was in prison for a very long time and denied conjugal visits, which I do believe is cruel and unusual punishment even though I have never been in jail other than that one night after my high school girlfriend made the mistake of telling her father that I had "a wicked tongue."

All other laws could use some regular breaking, if only to show why we have laws in the first place.

Which was why I broke into the home of Merry Martha McConklin the first time. I invaded the McConklin home the second through 20th time because I needed the money.

Merry Martha's piggy husband Morty McConklin, the restaurant toilet-paper king of South Chicago, was paying my daily fees plus expenses. Morty hated the thought of any stranger getting a little of Martha's strange, although in my line of work that was not so strange.

If Morty had his way, Martha would wear a huge sign saying, "No poaching. No trespassing. Vicious husband, hates sharing." And that sign would block all the possible and theoretical entrances to Martha, if you catch my drift.

What Morty wanted was perfectly focused pictures taken at night when his wife's theoretical activities became actual. How to accomplish this? Since I am a technical wizard, in addition to owning a yellow belt in karate, a brown belt in tai kwan-do, a puce belt in jujitsu and a pink belt of the master of chi throwing, I instantly knew that an ordinary camera was not up to the job. (In the interest of fairness and accuracy, I admit that I merely "own" those belts, having bought them at Killer Klothes 'r Us.)

The camera had to be motion sensitive, with infrared or at least 10,000 ASA capability to capture any activity in the semi-darkness. I rigged up a camera that I thought would do the job, attached the motion sensor so it would only snap pictures when something was moving and closed the blinds to my apartment to simulate night time.

I then put on various outfits to approximate Merry Martha's theoretical nighttime apparel. I tossed, turned and dry humped my bed, taking an entire roll of pictures. I guess by now you understand that I will do anything to satisfy a client.

When I had them developed, there were three rather instantaneous results: (1) the pictures were amazing in their detail, (2) I thought I looked rather good in them and (3) Jerry, the druggist's dyslexic son, asked if he could have a couple of copies of the pictures of me in the baby doll nightie with hose fastened by a black garter belt.

Naturally I was flattered, but I said no because they were part of an on-going case file.

The actual Merry Martha surveillance presented three difficult problems:

First, the camera had an audible "Click" whenever it took a picture. Would that click interfere or even halt activities in the bedroom? In other words, I asked myself: would hard dick stop for soft click? No, I said, because I figured, if the earth were moving, the participants might not notice a little click.

Second problem: when the roll was completely exposed, the camera automatically rewound and that significant sound lasted about seven seconds. I had to hope that the camera rewinding resembled a refrigerator making ice so it, too, would not be heard by Merry Martha and/or her suitor(s).

And third, I had to break into the house every day, remove the exposed roll and put new film in the camera.

On my first day on the job, I was able to place a camera in Martha's bedroom in the perfect position to get the in flagrante pictures that would earn me a bonus so large that it would allow me to stop living in my parents' weekend home.

Morty had promised that there would be triple pay for me if Martha were doing something with the unknown interloper that she had never done with or to Morty. When he said that, of course I questioned him at length because his offer considerably heightened my interest. I was never able to get an exact definition of what specific act would constitute an acceptable triple bonus. Our conversation went something like this:

ME: What if she's doing something with him with her mouth? Do I get paid triple then?

MORTY: No, I'm not sure, but I think she did that once a few years ago. I do remember that there were fireworks, so maybe it was on the Fourth of July.

ME: How can you not remember a blow job? I remember both of mine, including the one I gave myself. What about whips?

MORTY: No, that wouldn't qualify because once we used wet towels on each other in South Haven, Michigan, after a church retreat.

ME: That triple pay-off is sounding more and more like swamp land in Florida. Exactly what does get me the bonus?

MORTY: Hey, lay off. Think of me like that Supreme Court justice who defined pornography this way: I'll know it when I see it.

End of discussion.

Despite that appalling lack of definition, I set out to do everything I could to earn that triple bonus. I know, I know, sniffing after straying wives is not the most desirable work for the world's greatest detective, or at the very least the greatest detective living and working in Saw Mill, Michigan. Also, the only detective living and working in Saw Mill, Michigan.

Which gets me to the point in the story where I reveal how I got to Michigan and by extension into Merry Martha's bedroom, which will get us into my other big cases including the Case of the Softening Critics and The Case of the Nude Corpses Wearing Funny Shoes in My Parents' Living Room.

I don't know if I'll have time or the space to write in any detail about the Case of the Raccoon Who Went Sniffing, The Case of the Teens Pissing in the Woods or The Case Asking What Does the Caretaker Take Care Of When the

Caretaker Just Can't Take Care Of Himself. If not, as soon as I get a chance, I'll try to write about them on my web site-in-progress at www.world'sgreatestdetective.com

It all started, I suppose, when my wife Jennifer walked out on me. That sort of got the ball of my life rolling rapidly down hill as if my brakes were burned out and the steering wheel was locked while the radio played "Save the Last Dance For Me" as I careened into a garbage truck with a driver asleep at the wheel, if you get the picture.

One night, totally out of the blue (but after we had not spoken to each other or had sex for a full year), Jennifer completely surprised me by saying that she wanted someone taller, handsomer, more interesting and richer than I was. I made the mistake of yelling, "Well, no one's perfect."

Jennifer almost immediately announced that she had already found Mr. Tall, Handsome, Rich and Perfect. It was my best friend, Clarence "The Jukester" Cromwell, who was a shorter, fatter and I thought poorer man than I. When I pointed that out to Jen, she said, "Sticks and stones may break my bones, but Tony Testa ain't the besta," and left my life forever.

I later told Jukester that he was still my best friend because anyone who would take my wife off the market, when they were having a fire sale on the goods she was offering, would surely remain my best friend for the rest of time. Jukester, who later tried to remove my kneecaps, did not appreciate my gratitude.

And I'm not sure I meant it. Even as I said it, I was sure I would miss my wife's depressing hollow-eyed stare every time I took off my pants. I knew I would long for her grating voice each night when she yelled, "Tell me, Mr. Stupid Standing There with His Tongue Hanging Out, what don't you understand about the words 'No, asshole?'"

That same day I also had a somewhat serious economic reversal. I was fired and given no severance pay. And it wasn't like they were firing hundreds or even dozens of people at the same time. No, I was the only one shown the door that day.

I had been marketing vice president for crimescene.com, the first Internet company selling whatever was needed to process crime scenes. I had held that position for over six weeks, an employment longevity record at crimescene.com. We were the start-up that went through employees faster than Kaopectate going through a vacationer in Mexico after he won the taco eating contest.

The word came down that the upper management had decided that Tony Testa had no future. Specifically, Nate Gibson, the CEO with the dead man's eyes and the near-terminal dandruff, shouted at me in front of all three of our other employees, "Tony, you're history, scram."

Although Nate guaranteed me that my firing had absolutely nothing to do with my clever marketing ideas, I knew differently. My fortunes at crimescene.com went into precipitous decline after I convinced the company to sell actual murder weapons on the Internet.

I was in charge of marketing for one of the best crime sites on the web, an Internet location which blew through $23.5 million of venture capital faster than any other site in history except for that one that wanted to sell dog food and pooper scoopers with a hand puppet.

It was my job to figure out something we could sell to get some cash flow. The market for used cop uniforms with genuine doughnut stains was limited, so why not sell murder weapons? We could acquire the product, and there were people who wanted what we had to sell—in short, we were the perfect eCommerce solution.

That decision resulted in some unfortunate and unwanted publicity, especially after it became known that crimescene.com was getting the murder weapons from as-yet uncaptured criminals, who often used the money to purchase even more effective murder weapons.

8

In my defense, it never occurred to me that the weapons we auctioned over crimescene.com would be used again, or with such great effect. I thought people might like to have as harmless curios the cord with which John Wayne Gacy strangled 32 people, or the axe that Nellie Borden used when she gave her father "40 whacks," OJ's gloves and knife, and so on.

When the first dozen guns, knives, time bombs and vials filled with poison sold for over $1,450, we were happy campers. We broke out the Champagne and toasted the future. Crimescene.com was definitely showing income, it was dealing in actual "mortar," i. e. real goods, as opposed to just "clicks," i. e. Internet dweebs "clicking" on our site while looking for their nightly dose of porn. Nate Gibson even shook my hand and said, "Today, murder weapons; tomorrow, we arm the world."

How was I to know that those first dozen sales would lead to the three armed robberies and at least 11 new murders?

Crimescene.com attempted to recall all the murder weapons, which was tough to do since most of the poison was out of the vials, if you catch my drift. We quickly learned that people who buy poison over the Internet put it to good use minutes after grandma says, "I'm thinking of cutting you out of the will."

The financial press, ever eager to leap on any little bit of bad news especially when a formerly high flying company suffers a flesh wound in the proverbial scrotum, accused crimescene.com of trying to expand crime scenes throughout the world as a profit ploy.

Oh, to have been that clever--selling murder weapons so there would be more crime scenes, which would allow us to sell more mementos and create a geometric progression in our available inventory. But, alas, that was not the case.

However, I did have rather swift and sweet revenge. Just two hours after I was fired, crimescene.com was no more. The investors turned off the money spigot and the web site went dead. Anyone who was currently employed was sued by the board of directors for fraud and mismanagement.

The same day that I got fired and my wife left me (three being the charm especially where bad news is concerned), I was also wrongly evicted from my apartment. My landlady threw all my belongings into the street after my black Labrador, Mr. Jake the Clever Canine, yellow-streamed the landlady's baggy nylons. Mr. Jake expressed his urine-soaking dissatisfaction while she was complaining that Mr. Jake had eaten four pounds of cheese and a 27-pound frozen turkey in her refrigerator. Mr. Jake had trained himself to open almost any refrigerator that wasn't padlocked. I didn't name him the Clever Canine for nothing.

On the other hand, Mr. Jake was sick for a week after wolfing down all those calories, something that didn't bother my landlady one bit. She was a Yugoslavian woman who never bathed, had a serious mustache and was nicknamed "Tito's Revenge" by my fellow tenants. She was, in fact, quite threatening as she shouted, "He get good kick in ass he ever so much as gets near me, the sun o'bitch."

That was when Mr. Jake and me were thrown out on the sidewalk by the retarded sons of Tito's Revenge.

As I sat on the sidewalk amidst my belongings without an apartment, job or wife, I suddenly remembered that classic definition: home was where they always have to take you in.

Perhaps my parents had never heard of that rule. When I called them, I learned that my old room was no longer available because it had turned it into a gym. That was because Dad, a retired service station owner, had discovered the joys of using a stationary cycle while watching Susanne Sommers demonstrate the thigh cruncher on cable. Dad was a life-long, loyal fan of Susanne Sommers, whom he called that "kissable babe," a phrase my mother hated. He even enjoyed her Depends ads.

(Whenever I think of dad on his exer-cycle riding to nowhere while lusting after Susanne Sommers, I always have to ask myself who said that we all have to move through the gut of life like a small, wriggley mouse inside the snake of stupidity and forgetfulness? I have never gotten the answer to that question.)

Rather than living with them in a city that had been so cruel to me, my parents kindly suggested that I camp out at the family weekend cottage some 90 miles away, until I got my life straightened out or retired, which ever came first. (My dad was always a sarcastic son of a bitch.)

In the week before my marriage some nine months earlier, I had stayed with mom and dad in their apartment. It was a nice, family-friendly time until dad discovered that I was investigating his business practices.

For years dad had been paying off the ward supervisor so he could dump old oil in the sewers of his garage. Even back then, I was hoping to become a detective. That was why I hid in the bathroom of his garage and took pictures of the bribes being accepted and the yucky polluting stuff in his toilet.

Good old dad, who seemed to have more of an anger management problem the older he got, became very upset. I guess he reacted badly when I joked that he should give me a new car and $500 a week if he wanted me to keep the pictures to myself. Hey, I was only kidding! Dad's a big kidder, himself. Why else would he call me "a useless piece of shit?" Go figure.

Right after that argument was the first time my parents sent me alone to the family cottage in Sears Point just outside Saw Mill, Michigan, and it was probably why I was sent there most recently when I threatened to show up on their doorstep jobless, wifeless and homeless but with a terrific dog.

Mom, ever the polite mediator, again said as she did after I took pictures of dad bribing city officials, "We could look forward to visiting you in Sears Point every six months or so. Wouldn't that be special fun?"

Dad grumbled in a half-whisper, "Once every six years would be too often to see the bum." And that was that.

Since I was between jobs when I got to Sears Point, I figured it was time to live my dream full time. I wanted to be a gumshoe. I yearned to be just like the detectives in the movies or books. They all seemed to be hung over and angry all the time. And they had beautiful blondes falling all over them. Why couldn't I live that kind of life?

I'd made it my business to read nearly every detective book and see every detective movie, so I already knew lots of stuff about how a hard-boiled detective should operate. I had practiced sneering in front of a mirror, pretended to give and take good punches, and was able to drink a shot of bourbon with a cigarette in my mouth. What more did I need?

Hell, I'd even met a couple of real detectives who stopped by the apartment while they were investigating Uncle Guido's businesses.

I figured I'd open a detective office in my parents' home and begin living the life of my heroes. If the going got rough, I could always call on my Uncle Guido for help.

My parents' summer home was in Sears Point, a development just outside of Saw Mill on the shores of Lake Michigan. There were only 200 people living there full time, plus about 1,000 weekend or summer visitors and part-time owners. I figured it was a good place to start and, if I were at all successful, after a few months or weeks, I'd consider franchising.

The first thing I did was get some business cards printed up. These days you can't do anything without a business card. I decided that the cards would have this terrific slogan: "Private Eye / Public Detective." It was my way of telling people that I could keep my mouth shut, but that I'd still like their business.

12

Well, the local copy shop, which I have nicknamed "Klunko's," printed 200 cards with this slogan: "Private Eye / Pubic Detective."

The woman at the counter was nice enough to apologize and say that they'd do them over at no charge, but the more I looked at the slogan that Klunko's created, the more I liked it. Pubic detective. It might be telling it exactly as it was--that my detection work would be in the "pubic" area, what with divorces, straying husbands and randy wives.

With that single, brilliant typographical error, I would be able to accomplish what Coca-Cola and Pepsi, GM, Ford and Chrysler, Microsoft and Apple have spent years and millions of dollars trying to do—offer myself as a niche brand, separating myself completely from the competition and boldly announcing that my services would be utterly unique.

Any competitors in this area could be "private eyes." They might even become "public detectives." I would be the only "pubic detective."

Thanks to Klunko's, my niche in the market had been accurately and succinctly defined. I should have paid this erring copy store thousands of dollars. Instead, when asked if I wanted the business cards to be re-done, I merely mumbled, "Oh, forget about it," and walked out of the copy center.

So I kept the business cards the way they were. I pinned several of them on the Saw Mill "Age in Action" community center bulletin board on the theory that senior citizens can be as randy as anyone else.

The community center was actually a hallway in the Sears Point caretaker's home, which doubled as a place for mail boxes and a bulletin board. I was letting the people there know that there was a new detective in town.

Then my search for business took me into Saw Mill to talk to Clem Carlson, who'd been sheriff there for over 38 years. I figured that Sheriff Clem might be short handed with his three-person force and perhaps he could throw a little business my way.

One wall of Sheriff Clem's office was covered with pictures of surly characters staring out from ancient FBI information bulletins. Other walls had yellowing pictures of U. S. Presidents, state governors and local mayors. I looked back and forth. If I shifted my eyes very quickly, it was hard to know which were the crooks and which were the public servants. I tried to figure out what that might mean, but moving my eyes around that fast made me dizzy, so I stopped.

Sheriff Clem's desk was covered with so many papers, writs, warrants and candy wrappers that it looked like a candidate for a super fund environmental clean-up site. There were spittoons in every corner of the office. I glanced in one of them and I wished I hadn't. It bubbled with noxious liquid as if it housed a particularly repulsive alien.

Sheriff Clem hadn't changed in all the years I've known him. His huge love handles were still looking for love in all the wrong places, his hair-do resembled an over-used toilet brush, and a big wet cigar, clenched by his yellowed teeth, constantly drooped beneath his unkempt food-stained mustache. The only indication of the passage of years that I noticed was that today gray, instead of black, mustache hairs had strained the last bowl of chili he'd eaten.

Unfortunately, our conversation began on a sour note. Sheriff Clem took one look at me and immediately remembered a small, almost forgotten incident from my past. You'd think the guy would have forgiven a childish prank that had occurred on the weekend me and a couple of buddies graduated from high school. But, no, Sheriff Clem, who apparently has a memory roughly equal to that of a century plant, took one look at me and said, "I know you. You're one of the snot-nosed assholes who sank my boat."

I was about to explain once again (as I had so often in the past) that, even though we were high school students

14

and very drunk at the time, we did not sink his boat. Oh, my good friend Joe Pellicano did open some stopper or other in the bottom of the official sheriff's craft, which we all thought was hilarious at the time. But it was the water we let into his craft that sank his boat.

I explained that to him a decade ago, again a decade before that and almost every time I have set eyes on the man, but for some reason his mental powers simply could not accommodate to that idea.

I tried to divert his attention by denying the whole thing. I said, "Never heard of that incident. To quote George Bush the Elder during the Iran-Contra controversy, 'I wasn't in the loop.'"

But Sheriff Clem went back to memories of his boat, how it never ran right after the sinking, how his boat radio was all messed up and afterwards could only get lewd rock and roll from Chicago, and on and on.

I thanked him for his time and got out of there before he could remember anything more about me. When I was a sophomore in college, I had a beard for exactly one week and that, too, sometimes stuck in Sheriff Clem's mind. That conversation about the purported boat sinking was the first time in years that he didn't refer to me as "Tony, the bearded, bomb-throwing Bolshevik, tit-sucking asshole." I should be grateful for small favors.

A few days after my unfortunate interview with Sheriff Clem, my first client hired me. I guess putting up "pubic detective" business cards paid off more quickly than attempting to work with civil (or uncivil) authorities. It was that client, Morty McConklin, who came through with the job of watching Merry Martha.

Because of Morty's fervent desire for photographic proof, I was forced to enter Merry Martha's bedroom again and again to refresh the film in my almost hidden camera.

Because of the Madness of King Morty, I was discovered in the act of changing the film, which meant I was firmly in Martha's clutches. She then forced me to regularly return to her bedroom to get my pencil sharpened, my ashes hauled and my peanuts shucked. That was when Merry Martha diddled my kumquat, cleaned my plugs and points, and sucked my coils dry.

Not that I minded. Martha was one hot momma.

She told me over and over again that her husband was never able to understand her. Or satisfy her. After several years of marriage, she was more dissatisfied than a dentist with no cavities to fill and an expensive new drill that required monthly payments for the bank loan on the equipment. Morty, she complained, was good for a once-a-month jump start whether, as she put it, she needed it or not.

She called me her "Stud Muffin," which I found to be both irresistible and a very accurate description. Under Martha's constant ministrations, I was able to launch my rocket once every eight days without fail, which Martha assured me was way above average.

My torrid affair with my client's wife was far from problem free. If Morty ever found out what was going on, there was a high probability that he would attempt to kill me. After all, I was being paid by Martha's husband while I was charging the wife's batteries.

I weighed my options.

First, I needed the money, probably the most important consideration.

Second, I was getting close to the suspect, really close.

But then I thought: what if I had hired someone to check on my wife and he ended up bonking her? How would I feel?

In my life, my best friend, who had not been hired to do much of anything, was porking my soon-to-be ex-wife. I didn't like it and I couldn't do much about it. So I figured turn-around was fair play, what was good for that goose was good for this gander, and if the Jukester was having his ashes hauled, I could have mine without tying my shorts in knots.

Almost immediately, another dilemma occurred to me: should I tell Martha that I'm a private detective working for her husband and having her under surveillance?

Well, that was certainly a no-brainer. My immediate answer was: hell no.

Tony Testa's rule number one: let nothing interfere with the nooky, especially good nooky.

Tony Testa's rule number two: there is no bad nooky.

If I kept my mouth shut and played my cards right with only a little luck maybe some day Morty and Martha would want a little menagerie a trot, which is French for three people in bed at the same time and no one giggling.

This is something I've been thinking about for a while, but have never been able to figure out the social and physical engineering of that event.

In the past, any attempt at creating a menagerie a trot was hampered by what happened to Jerry Plumber, a friend of mine. He was married for over two years to a lovely woman, but he kept on complaining that marriage was very boring. "Scoring with your own wife," he said, "was like shooting fish in a barrel with a blunderbuss." So he and his good buddy began swapping.

Every Friday night, Jerry would go to his friend's house and nail his friend's wife, while the friend returned the favor. Now this is where the story gets kind of strange. In about a month, each woman began behaving exactly like the guy's real wife.

Jerry would be crawling into bed with his friend's wife and she would sneer, "Whom do you think is going to pick up that sock you just threw on the floor?"

She'd also complain that he forgot her birthday and she began having headaches on Jerry's Friday nights, and on and on. Meanwhile, in another room, Jerry's wife was giving his friend the same thing: nothing.

Jerry and his buddy figured that another couple would make the weekly event just perfect. So they introduced Steve Ratliffe and his wife into the mix. Steve's wife was an absolute knockout, a ten by anyone's reckoning. She had been runner up in the Miss Pittsburgh's a Wonderful Town Contest only about 15 years before her husband swapped her.

Steve, the energetic new guy, had his way with both Jerry's and his friend's wife, while the former Miss Pittsburgh's a Wonderful Town was making up her mind which guy upon whom to bestow her favors. It was an odd moment of indecisiveness on her part because it was assumed that before the night was out she would bed both, so what difference did it make--a point that Jerry and his buddy both tried to drive home, as it were.

Finally, the former Miss Pittsburgh's a Wonderful Town announced that she wanted nothing to do with either of them, that she found them both repugnant.

Jerry and his buddy were very disappointed and angry. They had traded their wives to this third guy, who took full advantage of the deal, while Jerry and his buddy were standing there with their mouths open and their dicks hanging out.

That Monday, Jerry and his buddy filed a law suit in the Cook County Circuit Court claiming that Steve had breached an unwritten contract and demanding $1,000,000 in reparations.

As you might suspect, a trial on those issues quickly became a complete circus. The former Miss Pittsburgh's a Wonderful Town testified that she found Jerry's penis to be "small, squat and ugly in the extreme," and the Chicago papers extensively quoted her.

The local alternative paper, the Reader, even had their court artist create drawings of what this penis might look

18

like. Because our lockers in the gym were often side by side, I can affirm that the artist was amazingly accurate.

(OK, so I also peaked at him when we were both taking a piss, but doesn't every guy do that?)

The law suit was thrown out of court. Then all three couples divorced. It put Jerry in a bad way date-wise because his private parts had been forever labeled as "small, squad and ugly in the extreme."

I mean, even if you were the most desperate divorcee in the world, would you want your friends to know that you are going out with a guy so labeled? I think not.

As far as Merry Martha was concerned, once she caught me, I was forced to continue "breaking in" to her home in the middle of the night so the neighbors wouldn't know I was enjoying her favors while Morty was working during the week in Chicago. The always inventive Martha was never asleep when I made my post-midnight forays. She often enjoyed playing "Catch the burglar," a game of her own devising in which she would "surprise" me by turning on the lights and holding me at gunpoint.

Having discovered the "theft in progress," she would have to discipline me. If I refused, she threatened to let her all-too-willing dog, Spyglass, out of the back porch. She even kept a can of Cheez Whiz handy. After she waved it in my face to emphasize her point, I would be forced to do whatever she wanted.

Let me explain:

Early in our relationship, during a casual conversation, Martha mentioned that when she was younger she enjoyed Cheez Whiz, but didn't care much for oral sex. Eventually she combined the two, achieving a sexual breakthrough at an early age.

She said, "By the time I got to college, I'd go through a case of Cheez Whiz a week."

Then she presented me with three large tubes of Cheez Whiz, told me to be creative and disappeared into the bathroom.

Feeling a little silly, I turned out the light and quickly sprayed a vast quantity of Cheez Whiz on the target area. As the old punchline said, it looked so good I almost ate it myself.

I was lying back, my eyes shut, expectantly waiting. Perhaps I was even getting a little impatient. After all, that cool, thick Cheez Whiz could very well cause my central magma chamber to erupt on its own if she didn't return quickly.

Only seconds later, Merry Martha lay her head on my thigh and her tongue began lapping at the Cheez Whiz--and me. Oh, joy; oh, pleasure; oh, golly, why hadn't I thought of the delight of Cheez Whiz before this?

My pleasure was growing and I wanted to let her share in the feelings. I reached out to stroke her back while whispering, "Martha, Martha, oh God, Martha, thank you."

That was when the door opened to the bathroom. There, silhouetted in the light, stood Martha, wearing only leather bikini underwear and a big smile. She said, "I see you've started without me."

I looked down and saw Spyglass, Martha's huge German Shepherd, furiously lapping at my crotch. I immediately sat up and tried to get away, but Spyglass put a huge paw on my stomach and pinned me down.

Martha suggested, "Just lie back and enjoy."

Well, I did attempt to relax. It wasn't all that easy because a huge, potentially vicious guard dog had his teeth around my family jewels. I think I also prayed that it would be quickly over, and mercifully it was.

Afterwards, Martha, who was always playful, offered me a milk bone or a doggie treat for being such a good boy.

From then on, whenever and wherever Spyglass saw me, he would immediately try to rush towards my crotch. If he were on a leash, Martha would pull him back while laughing so hard she could barely breath. If he was in the house, where he never was on a lead, he would put his front legs on my shoulders, drive me to the floor and attempt to stick his nose and teeth between my quickly crossed legs.

When walking my own dog, Mr. Jake the Clever Canine was no help at all. If Spyglass saw us, that dog would make a frantic bee-line for my crotch, while towing Merry Martha behind him. Jake would just stare at Spyglass with his head cocked to one side as if Mr. Jake were trying to figure out what kind of behavior this was. I hoped he wasn't thinking that he could learn something from Spyglass and that maybe snarfing at my crotch was something he wanted to do.

I continued to change Martha's film, so to speak, week nights from midnight to 5 am, guaranteeing that my weekly Morty stipend would continue. It was physically, but not mentally, demanding, amounting to less than a part-time job, but at least it got my foot in the door, so to speak, in the world of detecting.

I was dragging myself back to my parents' home at 5:45 one morning after Martha wanted to play the trapeze artist caught in the burglary. It was a game that required me to hang nude by my legs from a chandelier above her dining room table while trying to reach for a plastic peach on the dining room hutch. The peach represented the diamond I was trying to steal.

As I slowly limped home that night because my buttocks were quite raw from the punishment Martha meted out to the "burglar," I began thinking about the fact that all detectives I read about have girl friends who are real interesting--and none of them require the detective to hang nude from a chandelier.

One literary detective dates a whore, another is romantically involved with a doctor and Spencer in all the

Robert B. Parker novels is faithful to an oversexed therapist. If you could combine all of them, creating a whore-medical doctor-shrink, you might have the perfect woman. At the very least, you'd have someone adept at sex who could save you if you had a heart attack while in bed with her when she was wearing a 'Lil Bo Peep outfit. What an advantage that would be.

I, on the other hand, had no girlfriend at all, unless you count the woman who winked at me yesterday in the milk and yogurt section of the Piggly Wiggly.

In short, I was not in a very good mood when I unlocked the door to my parent's home, stepped inside and tripped over the nude body of a short, dapper man. I describe him as dapper because he wasn't completely nude. In fact, he was wearing some really nice moccasins.

He was lying on the floor of my parents' living room with his hands thrown over his head as if he had just kicked the winning field goal with two seconds left on the clock to give his team its first homecoming victory in half a century. And an arrow was stuck in his back.

I did what any hard-boiled, tough-guy, stronger-than-10-penny-nails detective would do. I screamed.

Allow me to explain that it this was not one of those little "eek-eek-oooo-yah" screams that sissies or weak-livered cowards offer when confronted with true horror. No, it was a full-throated, ripping from the gut, loud enough to wake the dead scream. A scream so forceful that it plunged me backward into the door frame, where I hit my head.

My skull throbbing, I staggered forward stunned as if I had been sucker-punched by an elephant in heat and I stepped directly on the guy's ass, which was still soft and fleshy.

It was just about the most disgusting thing that ever happened to me in my life. I mean, when I decided to become a detective, it never entered my mind that some dawn I would be grape-stomping the ass of a dead man.

Once I realized what I had done, I again totally creeped out. I was overcome with the fear that I would somehow fall through the body or that I'd get stuck inside it and would spend the rest of my years in the intestinal tract of a rotting corpse. Now that may seem like an unreasonable fear to you, my dear reader. But by then in my mind I had already taken up residence inside that corpse.

I fell to the floor with the result that my bugged-out eyes directly were staring at his bugged-out eyes. I would have screamed again, but I couldn't. I have to admit the truth here. I was scared proverbially shitless.

I touched the guy's cheek. That is, the one on the face. Soft, so he wasn't dead long. But cold. And definitely dead. At least, he wasn't yelling for me to get off his ass, something I assure you I would have done had our positions been reversed.

My next thought was "thank goodness." I mean, there was no requirement to attempt mouth-to-mouth resuscitation here. It's yucky enough to do that on a living person, especially if they are of the same sex. It would certainly be far ikkier on a corpse of the same sex. We have to be grateful for life's small favors.

Immediately after the scream, the fall to the floor, my examination of his facial cheek and the second, silent scream, my detective's brain began to work over time.

First conclusion: there was a dead man, which was untidy in the extreme, lying around my parents' living room and my mother was an excellent house keeper.

Second conclusion: if somebody used this guy for archery practice, that someone did not like this gentleman.

Third conclusion: Sheriff Clem doesn't like me and he'll probably blame me for the dead man no matter what I do now.

Fourth conclusion: my alibi -- that I was hanging nude from a chandelier in the Conklin manse at the time of the murder and I was doing that because I was afraid of a

German Shepherd that enjoyed licking Cheez Whiz off my balls -- would definitely not be backed up by Martha. Or believed by anyone in their right mind.

In addition, revealing what I was actually doing on this night might get me (a) killed by Morty or (b) sent to the electric chair with the executioners laughing while they zapped me on Super Fry.

Fifth conclusion: I need help. And fast.

So I called my Uncle Guido, the guy who said I should always call him if I was ever in a jam. I loved my Uncle Guido because, among other great attributes, he was my only relative who thought that becoming the head of marketing for crimescene.com was respectable, admirable employment.

He even helped in the endeavor. Uncle Guido was always able to tip me off to the latest in crime scene events, telling me where the bodies could be found and what sort of weapons might be grabbed if I got there fast enough. Sometimes I suspected that he had something to do with creating these crime scenes. I was flattered to believe that he was doing that because he wanted to make sure his nephew did well in his new job.

My Uncle Guido was there for me so consistently throughout my life that one day I asked my mother if Uncle Guido really was my father. Very enigmatically, my mother said, "Your Uncle Guido was a great dancer and that's all I'm going to say about that."

I remember seeing him at family get togethers and he always had some beautiful woman on his arm that he would introduce as "Bubbles, the newest aunt in the family." Sometimes they would be named "Tanya," or the unforgettable "Orgasm" (this was before anyone knew what that word meant), or "Jollies." All the men, except my father, would grin when Uncle Guido revealed their names. Maybe Dad was hoping that no one in the family would like the names enough to name their daughters after them.

One of my family's most deeply guarded secrets was that Uncle Guido was a well-connected mobster. At Christmas, Uncle Guido always gave the best presents, but I never quite grasped what Uncle Guido meant when he told my mother or father that this or that obviously expensive gift "just fell off Santa's sled."

I learned later that, during his long and unindicted life, Uncle Guido served as consiglieri to the powerful Carbonara family, which supposedly controlled south Chicago and its suburbs.

But disappointment was his frequent companion. His three sons, Primo, Secundo and Torvald, were soft momma's boys who proved to be totally unsuitable for following their father's successful footsteps.

Uncle Guido had hopes for Primo because in kindergarten Primo once dropped an eraser so he could look under the skirt of the teacher. When Uncle Guido was called in for a parent-teacher meeting about Primo, Uncle Guido proudly said, "That's my boy."

But Primo's early promise quickly faded away and, by the time Primo was in fourth grade, Uncle Guido's oldest son had won the spelling bee with the word "parole", was earning all A's and his report cards were peppered with notations proclaiming that "Primo gets along well with others."

Secundo and Torvald similarly disappointed their father, who often said that none of his sons were worthy of learning the business from him. He whispered to me on my 13th birthday that only I, his brother's first born, had the balls of a true Testosteroni.

Eventually, I began noticing that dad would always turn off the television just before the news featured the arrest of a covey of Mafiosi. I had to sneak out to my friend's homes to see my Uncle Guido walking into police stations with his fedora covering his face. Although Uncle Guido was arrested and investigated many times, he never spent an entire night in jail unless he needed an alibi.

In retrospect, I might have disappointed my Uncle Guido when I initially enrolled in college to study music with a major in the tuba. Uncle Guido half heartedly approved of my choice when I told him that I thought that I could use the tuba to make perfect farting sounds. My dream was to play "The Flight of the Bumble Bee" in a way that would cause bees to forget to make honey.

After one year, I switched to the business school, a move my Uncle Guido encouraged. He told me, "After all, the business of business is getting rid of competition any... way... you... can. Pretty soon, we'll be in the same business."

On the afternoon that I graduated from Chicago's Roosevelt University, Uncle Guido's associate, a man with cauliflower ears, sidled up to me, gave me a large, plain brown envelope, and whispered, "Special delivery from your Uncle Guido."

He quickly disappeared into the crowd and left me to explore the interior of that mysterious envelope. In it, I found an odd collection of cocktail napkins from dozens of fancy, now-defunct nightclubs.

Evidently written in the heat of hasty creativity and passion, often decorated with lip blots in various garish shades, and sometimes carrying the sopped up remains of various drinks, these cocktail napkins were the collected life lessons of my Uncle Guido. They were the best gift this college graduate could receive.

My uncle's philosophical observations included such deep thoughts as:

"Remember this: In any organization you are only one bullet from the top."

"Deal only in reality. Your enemies aren't dead until they begin to stink."

26

And, my favorite, "You can play Russian roulette without a pistol. It just means that winning takes longer and may ultimately be messier."

When I asked my uncle for an explanation of his cocktail-napkin graduation gift, Uncle Guido said, "Just call me your fuckin' obi wan cannoli." Then he winked, blinking back the sentimental tears that often came to his eyes. What an old softie!

I once I asked Uncle Guido for clarification of cocktail napkin number 38: "Wake up every morning and jump out of bed." And Uncle Guido said, "That's obvious. Either there's something out there that you better do right now or there's a severed horse's head in there with you. Whatever, getting out of bed fast is always a good idea."

Uncle Guido loved to remind me, "The best, and I might say only, way to go over the boss's head is if the head is six feet in the ground."

When I was in school studying for that business degree, I would often take my homework to Uncle Guido just to hear his wisdom.

I will never forget the time I told him that one business text noted, "If sleeping dogs lie too long, they will bite when awakened."

Uncle Guido, who always thought that anyone could learn more from dogs than from books, suggested additional lessons, including:

• If your fuckin' mutt bites me, I whack him, then I whack you, yuh dumb fuck.

• Only the lead dog gets a change of scenery. (I know this is an ancient management wheeze, but I do believe my Uncle Guido thought it up first. He always added, "All the other dogs must sniff the lead dog's ass.")

• The length of the leash determines where you shit.

• Being paper trained is the best way to end up on the New York Times.

27

• I'd rather lick my own balls than yours.

In short, my Uncle Guido was quite simply my perfect guru, my best friend and the relative I'd most turn to in times of trouble. So, when I tripped over a corpse in my parents' living room, I immediately called him even though he hated using the phone.

Uncle Guido answered with his normal phone conversation opener, "Talk. You got 10 seconds. Maybe less."

"It's Tony. I got a little problem."

Uncle Guido was abrupt, as he always was on the phone, "Where are you? Ask me a question."

"Where did the sheriff's boat sink?"

The line went dead. Uncle Guido had all the information he needed to find me.

During the hour or so I had alone with the corpse until Uncle Guido arrived, I was able to identify the body. It belonged to Jerry Andrews, current president of the Sears Point Home Owners and Land Trust Deed Holders Association.

When he was alive, this former Whirlpool claims adjuster was a human replica of the Esquire Magazine trademark; a short, dignified, rather jaunty man with a precisely trimmed white mustache. Jerry was a guy who would have looked comfortable in a cutaway tux with spats and a striped vest.

I easily recognized him because Jerry was the first Sears Point adult over age 45 to wear Speedo trunks to the beach. This was an event we teens talked about a lot because those trunks confirmed one persistent Sears Point rumor: that Jerry Andrews was the best hung man at the shore. I mean, this guy had a basket on him anyone could hit from beyond the three-point line with his or her eyes closed.

The kids whispered that he had to fold his mighty member in half to get it inside his Speedos, but that wasn't true, especially after he had taken a swim in the often chilly Lake Michigan waters.

Because I am a trained observer, I immediately noticed that Jerry Andrews had died with his flag at full staff, with his rod way out there casting, his sword prepared to joust. His stand-up erection was such that, even if I had wanted to, it would have been impossible to roll Andrews' body out of the living room.

Uncle Guido finally arrived with Pro, his associate, back up, constant companion, and bodyguard. It was Pro who had handed me Uncle Guido's collected cocktail napkin wisdom on my graduation day.

Earlier I mentioned that he had cauliflower ears, but there was more to him than that. Pro is a mountain of a man, a cunt hair under six and a half feet tall, weighing in at around 385 pounds with hands big enough to make bowling balls look like tiny aspirins.

I never knew Pro's first or last name, or even what Pro stood for. It could be short for "professional" or "prodigious," although I doubt that the Organization's vocabulary was up to a complicated nickname. It could even have been "proctologist," although Pro never showed any talent for that branch of medicine other than to occasionally mutter that he would love to "ream a new asshole" for someone who upset him.

The usually silent Pro entered the cottage, saw the dead man on the floor wearing moccasins and said, "Ugly shoes."

The next comment came from my Uncle Guido, who upon seeing Jerry's resplendent mast, commented, "What a schlong. That's a putz to be proud of."

Thus proving that my Uncle Guido could be as generous with his compliments as he was outspoken with his criticisms.

Uncle Guido asked, "So who's the owner of the boner that's the subject of your phoner?"

"That's Jerry Andrews," I said. "Nice guy, loved his wife. Even had a second toilet put in his master bathroom so they could sit side by side."

Pro asked, "What kind of guy wants to take a crap with his wife? If I'd a known that was going on, I'd have shot the little shitter myself."

"Actually, more of a big shitter," I pointed out. "He was on an all-fiber diet for most of his life. He often only ate raw cabbage for weeks at a time."

Uncle Guido observed, "I bet it didn't work."

"Oh, he lost a lot of weight and was bragging about the diet book he would write," I said. "But then there was the gas problem. People would walk around his house in a large arc. Then he started complaining about the bleeding."

Pro added, "Tough to sell a diet that makes you fart and bleed from the ass."

My reasonable Uncle Guido said, "Oh well, one man's dream is another man's disgust."

Once again I wished I had a pencil and a notebook to write down Uncle Guido's wisdom as he uttered it. I can think of no greater honor than to be my Uncle's Boswell, but I don't think he would stand for it. I knew that the moment I told him about Boswell, Uncle Guido would call him "the squealer," and that would be that.

Uncle Guido turned to me and asked, "You weren't thinking about calling any cops, were you?" He said that ominously and the implication was that, if that notion had even flitted through my mind, it might mean that I was no longer a member of his family in good standing.

"No," I answered quickly, "Sheriff Clem and I haven't gotten along very well for the last 18 or 19 years."

30

Uncle Guido smiled, clapped me on the back and proudly said to Pro, "That's my nephew. Ain't he the greatest?"

Pro seemed pre-occupied about the body in the living room. He asked, "What you figure? We take him to the dump? Think the rats need a good meal?"

Uncle Guido said, "Forget about it. There's always someone going through dumps these days. Homeless people, artists finding objects, environmentalists. It's not like the old days when only bears and rats went to dumps." Uncle Guido sounded almost wistful.

"Any highways being paved? Anyone pouring concrete or creating end zones around here?" Pro seemed to know lots of places to put bodies. I just kept quiet and let the experts work things out.

Uncle Guido got a little exasperated, "We might want the body in the future. You want to go digging through a foot of concrete highway or end zones at midnight to bring this prick back?"

Pro's face showed disgust. At least I think it was disgust. Might have been indigestion.

Then Uncle Guido began thinking out loud, "We just need to store him for a while until we figure out who didn't like the naked Tonto over there. Then we produce him, let the cops collar the doer, get my nephew out of their cross-hairs, and none of these locals will be any the wiser."

After several minutes of serious concentration, he snapped his fingers and yelled, "I got it. Tony, your parents got a freezer, don't they?"

Sure they did. And a big one, too. Every six months or so, they'd buy an entire side of beef. Then dad would boast that he laughed at meat prices all the way to the freezer.

So we all--except the very dead Jerry, of course-- trooped down to the basement and emptied the freezer.

While we were in the middle of the job, Uncle Guido asked me to hand him a frozen turkey. He read the label, "Says here defrosting takes a half hour per pound, unless you put the turkey in water. It says you have to constantly change the water. Any of you guys want to do that?"

I ask, "Why worry about defrosting a turkey?"

Uncle Guido gave me a loving smack on the back of the head and answered, "If we decide to suddenly let the authorities find the body, it can't be not-so-fresh frozen or they'll suspect something's amiss."

Pro muttered, "Yah, like how many fresh frozen corpses do they get around here?"

I thought they might find a few during the winter, but I kept that to myself.

Uncle Guido did some fast figuring, "Say he's 150 pounds, that's 75 hours or a little over three days at room temperature. And we'll have to be careful when we take him out of the freezer not to break off his pecker. No way anyone could explain that."

My Uncle Guido was a guy who always saw the angles that other people didn't.

After we emptied the freezer, Pro carried the body downstairs. Then he slipped the plastic cover from the Sunday New York times over Jerry's erect member to protect it. Jerry Andrews looked like an irate newspaper deliveryman had stabbed him in the crotch.

Uncle Guido said that Mr. Andrews would only become ripe if we lost power for more than a week, which we agreed was unlikely. I found a padlock and secured the freezer to make sure no nosy Nellies could accidentally look at Mr. Andrews.

We were all pretty satisfied with our temporary solution until I looked around and saw the piles of meat that we had to take out of the freezer to make room for Mr. Andrews. When I commented that a lot of that would spoil, Uncle

Guido said, "Fug-get-about-it, eating meat ain't that good for you anyways."

Pro whispered, "You could have a bar-b-que?"

"Pro, you're a genius," Uncle Guido enthused. "Have it tomorrow, before the meat spoils. Then we can check out the locals to see if one of them offed Mr. Well Hung. Right now, let's have a couple of steaks and talk about what's next."

Despite the fact that I'd spent the night hanging from Merry Martha's chandelier and that the morning was pretty much ruined when I stepped on a dead body, I forgot my exhaustion, fired up the grill and made the steaks. But I have to admit that I was a little peeved.

I'd called Uncle Guido because I was in trouble. Yes, the body was no longer in the living room, but it was turning blue in my parents' freezer. Instead of doing something about my situation, Pro and Uncle Guido were sitting down and waiting for me to cook for them.

It was certainly not what I expected when I called my esteemed uncle. I thought at the very least some legs would get broken and my problems would disappear.

Instead Uncle Guido was spending the morning suggesting that Pro learn to express his feelings. Uncle Guido advised, "That's why you can't score with no broads-- they want touchy-feely shit and all you can give them is three .45 slugs in the heart from 50 yards away. Don't take me wrong. I admire your expertise with a gun, but it don't make a chick want to get naked with you, if you understand my drift."

I took the steaks off the grill and wrote a mental memo to myself to learn more about touchy-feely shit.

As soon as we sat down to breakfast, Uncle Guido turned to me with a serious expression, "You do know that guy was whacked as a message to me."

"With all due respect to you, my beloved uncle," I began, "Jerry Andrews had a lot of enemies."

"Like who?"

"For one, he didn't want a tennis court put in and all the younger owners did. As president of the association, he would certainly be in charge of the next general meeting. With him gone, that tennis court might get built."

"Tony, Tony, Tony," my Uncle Guido said, putting his hand on my forearm and stopping me from forking a big hunk of steak into my mouth. "Are you telling me he was killed over lobs and love and tiny white skirts and guys who are proud of looking like sissies? Excuse me, but that makes as much sense as believing that the Cubs will win the World Series while any of us are alive!"

He sounded so disappointed in me that I could only say in my softest voice, "Tennis courts are very important around here. It's been a tough battle and neither side was giving an inch."

"Do you know anything else about this guy?"

"Nothing," I said, "Other than what you saw. He was apparently well endowed."

Pro interrupted, "The most impressive package since Dillinger."

I was amazed that a man like Pro was so well informed about history, but then he was talking about his hero.

"So you're saying that his fly might have been a lending library?"

"Let me put it this way, Uncle Guido. Half the children born to year round residents of Sears Point were short people, like Jerry Andrews. Both the boys and girls had trim little mustaches by the time they were 15 years old."

Uncle Guido reluctantly agreed, "So, all we gotta do is find out who he was porking, look at the husbands and, badda-bing, we got you off the hook. This detecting business is all right."

Pro added, "Don't forget the shoes. We should find a broad what wants to get laid by Geronimo."

I added, "And angry tennis players."

Uncle Guido was smiling and saying, "And guys who want to send me a message. This whole thing is beginning to give me a headache."

Then the phone rang. It was Martha, who wanted me to come over immediately so we could play Hide the Salami, a new game she claimed she just made up.

Despite the barking of her dog, Spyglass, I fell asleep as she was going over the rules which weren't all that complicated as I remember them.

Chapter Two

Forget the slogan "Build it and they will come."

That saying was from that Kevin Costner movie in which he stashed the ghost of his father in a cornfield and almost everyone who watched the movie got all weepy. All I could think about was: what kind of grown kid lets his father wait around in a corn field since 1934? I thought the movie should have ended with the guys in the white outfits putting Costner in a straight jacket, tossing him in the back of an ambulance and taking him away as all the ball players from the field throw corn cobs at him.

To me, the slogan to remember was not "Build it and they will come." It was: "Provide free food and you'll surely attract a big crowd."

That turned out to be sure-fire wisdom. When it came time for my "Eat Meat Before It Spoils" bar-b-que at sunset the next day, nearly everyone in Sears Point showed up. Some local pastor should have created a sermon titled, "The Miracle of the Frozen Rib Eyes: The Theological Implications of the Freebie."

People came that had been bedridden for the previous eight years. Agoraphobics who always sat quivering behind their closed blinds went blinking into the sunset for the first time in decades, attracted as they were to the smell of slabs of dead meat on a fire. Vegetarians broke their vows and hermits became social beasts. If the bar-b-que were in Chicago, the dead would have risen, not to vote, but to scarf down the free food.

It didn't really matter that the meat hadn't quite defrosted. It was eaten anyway. Hell, it wouldn't have mattered if the meat were green or smelled like limburger cheese. People just kept on plunking chickens and beef on the grill, slathering them with bar-b-que sauce, and announcing, "You city folks sure do know about new dishes."

One of my guests cracked a tooth on the still-solid, cold and crunchy center of a steak, but continued to eat despite the pain.

Of course, Sheriff Clem was there, looking at everyone suspiciously as if he was still trying to figure out who had sunk his boat a quarter of a century ago.

Sheriff Clem squinted in my direction, sauntered over to me and asked if we'd seen "hide nor hair" of Jerry Andrews. Clem explained that old Jerry had apparently "gone missing" a couple of days ago and his wife Bertha was beginning to get concerned.

36

I tried to ask in a most innocent manner, "Why are you asking me? I haven't seen the man since last summer."

"Well, Antonio," Clem said, spatting a wad of tobacco into mom's blooming double-red impatiens, "I need to talk to you man to man -- and this should go no further."

After I agreed, Sheriff Clem opined, "You see, it was pretty well known around here that when Jerry wanted to stray from the corral and frolic with some strange heifer, he'd use your folks' home as his humping grounds."

When I looked shocked, Sheriff Clem quickly added, "I think he had your dad's permission, but in any case, he said he always washed the sheets. And he never forgot to take home the Grover Washington album that Jerry said was so effective with the weaker sex. You see, pretty much everyone knew about Jerry's arrangement and that's why, when Bertha said he hadn't shown up, I figured maybe he went to sleep in your place. He didn't, did he?"

I quickly (hoping it was not too quickly) said that he hadn't. That took care of that problem, except for a nagging thought that came to mind. Just last summer, when I was talking to Sheriff Clem's teen-aged daughter, Melanie, she had commented at length and in depth about the outline of Mr. Andrews' tentpole when he wore his Speedos to the beach.

Melanie, a sweet, but not-so-innocent local teenager, had squealed, "Why, that man is hung like a horse."

Had Melanie acted on that curiosity? If so, had Sheriff Clem heard of Jerry's poaching on the law officer's alleged virginal daughter? Wouldn't that give Sheriff Clem more than enough of a motive to kill Jerry?

Note to self: these are good questions, but upsetting to Sheriff Clem. Is there anyone I can convince to ask these and other questions of the Sheriff?

Elmer Omittus, my parents' plumber, was also in attendance at the bar-b-que. When I am 94, as Elmer was, I too want to eat six Polish sausage sandwiches with sauerkraut, raw onions, pickles and mustard and suffer no stomach problems.

Ever since Elmer accepted that emergency plumbing job at the local nuclear plant, Elmer and I had been greeting each other with friendly jokes. At the bar-b-que I said, "Hi, Elmer. I hear your wife can't sleep because you glow in the dark."

"You got it right, buster," he cackled. "I'll bring over my light saber so you can hold it and read by it. Maybe tonight?"

Before I could stop laughing and say, "No, thank you," Uncle Guido said, "You the plumber? I find it always pays to be friendly to the local plumber, if you catch my drift."

Then Uncle Guido crossed his forefinger under his nose and winked. He added, "We'd like to hear what you know about that guy Jerry whatshisname, the president of this cow pasture."

"Not much to tell," Elmer said, without a moment's hesitation. "Everyone hated him. Especially me. He criticized my plumbing after he bonked my wife. A fellow shouldn't oughta do both--criticize and screw. One would be enough for any man, wouldn't you think?"

We agreed. At that point, as the fat hit the coals causing the grill to flare once again, Jim and Dottie Gerlund sidled up to me and asked if they could speak to me privately.

The Gerlunds, who lived in a wood-shingled house atop King's Roost, the tallest hill/dune in Sears Point, were reputed to be a most contented couple. Jim was wearing his usual madras Bermuda shorts, one of the dozen he purchased during a trip to Sioux Ste. Marie, Michigan, in 1967. Dottie was at his side looking, as she always did, like the model for the grandmother in a television commercial extolling the best soup on a cold day. Her looks could be deceiving.

As I gazed at Jim, I realized that he might be still angry about losing a close election for the association presidency to Mr. Andrews. Things got so heated during the brief

38

campaign that, if I remember correctly, Jim threatened to murder a famous resident of Sears Point. At the time, he claimed that Chad Parkington, a local movie critic on television, had illegally affected the results. I wasn't quite sure what Jim thought had happened. But it was widely whispered that Jim had muttered that some day, when Jim got his mitts on Chad, Jim would "Give new meaning to the phrase 'hanging Chad.'"

It was rumored that Jerry had also put the blocks to Dottie at one time or another, meaning that Jim was certainly another a suspect.

Jim, a good natured guy with a smile as big as the Mississippi drainage system, had known me since I was eight years old. Whenever he saw me, he always performed the same trick. Jim Gerlund would wave his hands dangerously close to my eyes, making confusing fluttering motions to distract me. Since I have known what was coming next for nearly the last three decades, I was almost never distracted.

Jim would then produce a quarter by pretending to grab my ear and plucking it out of my Eustachian tubes. Then he'd say the same thing he'd said every time since he first met me, "Tony, you've got to do a better job of cleaning your ears."

I always smiled as he reminded me that I should take a wash cloth to my ears before my mother did. Then Jim would try to give me the quarter, which I would refuse by folding my hands under my armpits and expressing a firm determination not to accept the two bits from this pest.

Jim would smile, say, "Aw, shucks, look who's embarrassed?"

Then he would do what he always did and put the quarter down the back of my shirt or shove it into the front of my pants. It would sit in my underwear until I dug it out later that night.

When I was younger, I would always boil the quarter before spending it. Now I generally saved up a lot of them and hurled them at the Gerlunds home late at night in the hopes of giving that crazed one-trick magician a heart attack.

Before I could respond to the Gerlunds' request for a conversation, George Svaboda joined us. George, the friendly fellow who cut dad's grass when we weren't in Sears Point, was proudest of his truck, his wife, and his son, quite possibly in that order. When he, too, asked if he could see me for a quiet conversation, I figured my private eye business was really looking up.

Only about a week before my cook-out, Jerry Andrews had accused George of poisoning Jerry's rose bushes with the wrong aphid spray. If the folks in Sears Point believed that, George's yard maintenance business was over. People don't take kindly to rose bush killers in these parts. It was a dispute that definitely made George another suspect.

That was the first time it occurred to me that, rather than coming up with a list of all the locals who might have a motive for killing Jerry, it might be easier to come up with a short list of anyone who didn't want to kill him.

While I was deciding if I should spend quality (meaning, profitable) time with the Gerlunds or Svaboda, The Blonde slinked up to me. She was tall. She was gorgeous. She was blonde like a wheat field yearning to be fondled and ravaged, blonde like the aging teeth of a courtesan accustomed to toppling heads of state, blonde like the stream of urine cast into the trough of the men's washroom at Wrigley Field after six beers and a surprising Cubs win. In other words, she was blonde.

When The Blonde mentioned that she preferred speaking to me in my bedroom, the decision was pretty much made for me. I told the Gerlunds and Svaboda that we could continue our conversations in a few minutes.

Like all good detective novels, movies and maybe even many real-life crime stories, my next great case began with

40

that Blonde. That's why I call this case The Blonde With The Big Memories.

My lady visitor sat on the easy chair in my parents' bedroom after throwing to the floor a large pile of Playboy and Hustler magazines. I quickly explained that I was saving the Playboys because I enjoyed reading the stories, but I do not think she believed me. I didn't bother to explain the Hustlers.

She crossed her legs and I could immediately detect that they went all the way up to there and then some. They were the legs you'd write sonnets on, if you were a poet and if she let you get that close to her and if she didn't mind a lot of ink on her inner thighs. The first moment I set eyes on those legs I began thinking that, if only I had a gallon of peach preserves, some whipped cream, a quart of maraschino cherries and a pint of Ben and Jerry's chocolate fudge, those legs and I could have a really great time.

She had a come-hither look which was so high wattage that it verged on a come-as-quickly-as-you-can smile. Her lips were thick and inviting, moist and only half shut. They were the kind of lips you'd love to see surrounding a raspberry Popsicle on a hot summer's day.

She definitely had cleavage, showing off the kind of cantilevered, protruding mounds that give Almond (and all my nuts) so much Joy. Her perky, insouciant breasts were standing at attention and were crying out for a good nuzzling by yours truly.

She was wearing a tiny hat with a veil that did nothing to hide her bedroom eyes. (This was unusual garb for a neighborhood bar-b-que but expected of any Blonde who entered any detective's bedroom.)

Put all that together on a five-foot 10-inch frame and you have the girl the world would most love to canoodle; a walking, breathing object of desire; a living sex fantasy for all the Vaseline and pillow fights of my dreams.

Then, as if Mr. Jake the Clever Canine was the extension of my most fetid, fervid, frantic fantasies, he ran in to the bedroom, put his nose directly into her lap and began humping her leg.

I tried to be nonchalant about my beloved pet doing what I so wanted to do. Using my best off-hand, insouciant manner, I said, "Oh, Mr. Jake, aren't you carrying hospitality a little far?" Then I laughed, hoping that she would understand that I wasn't actually complimenting my "Bad, bad doggie."

She merely lifted one leg, giving both Mr. Jake and I a glimpse nearly to heaven's gates, and shoved Mr. Jake away. When he made a move to resume his passion position, she looked sternly at him and quietly, but forcefully said, "No." Mr. Jake slunk away, a deflated male who acknowledged that there was the new alpha in his world.

I knew I needed to get control of this situation, so I sneered at her, letting one side of my mouth quiver like one dog smelling another's asshole. It is good to let women know who is boss from the very beginning. I asked, "What brings you here, honey cakes?"

With that, she uncrossed her legs, stood, and walked towards me. I thought she was going to kiss me--that's the way it would happen in a Mickey Spillane novel, but the Mick would never include the part about the dog humping her leg. Spillane was tough, but he wasn't tough enough to reveal the complete truth.

Instead of kissing me, she slapped me. Hard enough to rattle my teeth and bruise my brain. Before I could say, "Hey, what gives?" She recited a little Dr. Seuss-type rap:

"I am not your honey

I am not your bunny

If you think that's funny

You'll never get my cunny."

Or words to that effect. I would have laughed except that my jaw was beginning to swell.

Keeping my tough-guy facade, despite the fact that my face had been re-arranged, I sneered, "Tho, what'th on your mind, thith-ter?"

Fearing another slap, I quickly amended the "Sister" to, "Mith? Mithes? Lady?"

"Just call me Amanda," she said, adding, "We need your help, Shamus."

No one had ever called me a "Shamus" before. It felt good. Real good. Shamus was an antiquated word found in many detective books of the '30s and, from my reading, I thought that it meant "A tough detective who eats five-day old bagels without breaking a tooth" or something like that. It might also refer to the old guy who cleans up Jewish temples, but I was sure Amanda wasn't talking about that.

"Depends on who is the 'we,' what is the 'help,'" I lisped.

She sighed, which expanded her healthy, cantilevered garbanzos to eye-popping proportions, and then she intoned, "I need your undivided attention. Could you stop thinking with your cock for just one minute?"

Not the easiest request, but something a super detective like me can do. I looked directly into her eyes for, oh, maybe the next 22 seconds.

Amanda continued, fetchingly, "I produce the TV show Three Guys at the Movies. You know, the critics who say every new film is crap?"

Of course I knew. The Three Guys were famous. One of them, Chad Parkington, the height challenged critic, was actually a full-sized dwarf (at least that's what his publicity releases claimed), half a whisker over four feet tall. He was an angry, vicious little man willing to bite the ankle of anyone who noticed that he was short. He never gave a positive review to any movie starring tall people. Once Alan Ladd, the famously height-challenged star of the '40s, stopped making new films, Chad could not find a movie or a star he loved.

Chad had a weekend home in Duneland Estates, not far from Sears Point. It was rumored that his ceilings were only five feet tall and the toilet was less than eight inches off the floor, making it an uncomfortable place for anyone of close-to-normal height to do his or her business.

The obese Trey Parker, who gave bad reviews to any movie starring thin people (meaning nearly every film produced by Hollywood), was another panelist. Parker ardently defended "Naturalistische Film Making," his theory that all good films must be without edits or cuts, lighting, make up, script or direction. He wasn't sure that film should be put in a camera, preferring to invite the audience out to witness real life. As far as I knew, Trey Parker was the only person in the world who believed in his theory, which would have severely diminished the popcorn sales in theaters.

The third panelist was the looks-challenged Freddie Niles, who often received invitations to "come as you are" Halloween parties with the additional notation of "but not you, Freddie." Most people thought that Freddie hated films because they usually starred beautiful people, but that wasn't completely true. His deep negativity began at the age of five when his parents took him to see "Frankenstein" and more people in the audience were frightened of him than of Boris Karlov.

The Three Guys was an extremely popular show and it wasn't difficult to figure out why. They were a trio of less than ordinary people who delighted in destroying the artistic efforts of those who were much better fed, prettier and, yes, more talented then they were. It was the revenge of the underclass, the attack of the uglies.

"The problem is Chad," Amanda continued, sexy in her seriousness. "For the last month he has loved every movie he's reviewed."

"What's so bad about that?"

"Every movie, including 'Showgirls 2: In Search of Their Lost Virginity.'" She sighed and my heart--and a lot of my id--went out to her.

But I still didn't fully understand the gravity of the situation. "So he gets off on that stuff. So what?"

Amanda began to get impatient, "One, 'Showgirls' was, by definition, about tall women with long legs. Chad hates tall women, but he drooled over this movie. He loved the scene in which the star of 'Showgirls 2' went back to her old nightclub and her old boss said, 'Now that you're at the Desert Storm, the fancy, expensive club, it must be nice that people don't cum in your hair every night.' It was the same line they used in the first 'Showgirls' film. Chad thought the line illustrated, and I'm quoting, 'The underlying pathos of the upwardly mobile worker in a heartless society.'"

Amanda shook her head in dismay.

I opined, "There might be a simple, scientific explanation. Chad could have either gone soft in the head or hard in the dick. Why would you need the services of a detective to find out why Chad suddenly likes movies?"

She looked like a dove that showed up at a peace conference without its garlic clove or whatever doves carry in their mouths. She whined, "There's more, but I can only tell you if you promise to keep it a secret."

"Promise," I said, although I knew I could never keep quiet about anything she told me or, if my prayers were ever answered, did to me.

"Cross your heart and hope to die?" Amanda was so cute when she was trying to negotiate a deal.

"Cross my heart," I repeated, although I never knew why those words would ever seal anyone's lips.

"Swear on your mother's grave?"

Now she was getting tedious, so I harrumphed, "I'll swear on your mother's grave. Get on with it, what the hell do you have to tell me?"

"Chad Parkington is missing."

Her gravity seemed ridiculous to me. I asked, "He's small. Have you looked in all the drawers? He could be hiding behind something or crouching down somewhere. I'm sure he'll turn up when he's hungry."

"No, you don't understand," she said impatiently. "This is no game. Chad Parkington has actually disappeared."

"Since when? I saw him on the show just last weekend."

Amanda was wonderfully patient as she explained the situation to me. As she spoke, all I could think of was that she would be the perfect partner for someone with premature ejaculation problems -- not that I have that malady, but if I knew someone who did, I'd send him to her.

She whispered, "You are probably referring to TV images seen from behind his head during the last few shows. For those pictures, we had a substitute sitting there. Just a silent, short actor wearing his hair the way Chad did. You and everyone else at home only saw the back of his head."

I was not convinced and I started to say, "But I heard him say..."

Amanda told me, "What he always says. 'The movie is crap.' 'The worst movie ever put out by a major Hollywood studio.' They were recorded comments from shows first seen three to five years ago, plus some off camera ad libs we had never broadcast. We wanted to keep him fresh."

"And I saw his face, right there, on camera...

Amanda said, "At those times he was waiting to speak, anxious to get his two cents in. You saw him say nothing, only react to what others were saying. His close ups were shots from earlier shows. Chad always wears pretty much the same thing every week, so there was no problem with his wardrobe giving away the fact that we're creating a virtual Chad."

46

She carefully explained that, because of rising costs and the desire for more profits, all the owners of television series have wanted to figure out ways to eliminate actors, anchors and stars. In the short term, Chad actually did the station owners a favor by disappearing so they could experiment with what they hope to do in the future.

"But now we're on the last of his surprise ad libs," Amanda revealed. "This has been going on for three months."

I was amazed. "Three months!"

"Some day the word will get out and the show will die. We need to find the real Chad and fast."

I had to ask, "So when Chad disappeared, did you replace him with the old, negative Chad or the new, love-everything Chad—the Chad with a hard-on for 'Showgirls' sequels?"

Amanda seemed amazed that I would ask the question. She scoffed, "The old Chad, of course. If you were going to clone Elvis, would you bring him back as the young, skinny stud or as the older, bloated joke? Anyway, the new nice-guy Chad was awful. He was killing himself and the show."

"I want you to find Chad or his body," Amanda continued. "If he's alive, I want you to bring back the old Chad who shit on everything in the movies. I will double your fee if you can accomplish this in a week."

Suddenly the mystery of the uncritical, disappearing critic seemed a worthy challenge for my talents. When we shook hands on the deal, I quickly rubbed my middle finger along the lifeline of her palm as a subtle signal that I was interested in so much more than a handshake.

Amanda completely understood my seductive gambit. She put both her hands on my shoulders and drew me closer to her. I was sure she was going to kiss me to get the ball rolling.

Then she kicked me in the groin and asked, "Let's keep this strictly business. Any problem with that?"

When I found it difficult to answer her, she left me wheezing on the floor, holding my tenderlys.

I was falling in love.

When I rejoined the bar-b-que, no one commented on the fact that I was walking bent over. It's amazing that non-detecting civilians notice so very little about their fellow men.

Before I could return to Svaboda and the Gerlunds, Merry Martha came up to me, grabbed my biceps and whispered, "My salami is missing. Do you understand? I need to find my salami and I want it right now."

Martha was always subtle. Anyone overhearing our conversation would think that she was referring a sandwich or a deli treat. I knew differently.

I would have immediately joined her except for two considerations: it was my party and the guests were about to bar-b-que a dozen semi-frozen chickens. Also, Amanda's love tap had shriveled my interest in salami placement for the time being.

So I told Martha that I would provide her with my own salami as soon as I could, certainly before the next millennium. I thought it was a pretty good way of handling her needs, although I was disheartened to hear her whisper the word "Asshole" as I left her.

Women are so fickle and mysterious, aren't they?

I limped back to rejoin the Gerlunds, who seemed anxious to see me. Before she said anything, Dottie Gerlund looked both ways to make sure no one was listening to us. Then she tugged on my sleeve and brought my ear down so it was level with her mouth.

She asked, "This is very important. Have you heard about the goings on at the Clement house?"

She also tended to slurp on her "S" sounds when she spoke. Fortunately my training as one who could ignore his bodily needs for hours at a time allowed me to continue listening without drying my ear. If I had succumbed to the need to mop my aural canal, which was being flooded by Dottie's spittle, I'm certain it would have distracted her and I might never have heard the end of her story.

As it was, she steam-rolled onward, "You know Mrs. Clements, the divorcee?" She pronounced the word "Dee-vyor-say" and her tone indicated a Mount Everest of disapproval.

Jim, meanwhile, was standing just behind his missus, waving and winking at me in a slightly apologetic manner, indicating that he would share no honey from whatever bee was currently in her bonnet.

"The problem is that Mrs. Clements's son sneaks in to her house. You remember him?" She asked. Responding to my blank look, Dottie continued, "He's the one who went to jail for a week for drunk driving and urinating on Officer Todd Brown's new uniform pants a year ago New Year's Eve." Dottie said.

"Even so," I commented, "I would think the boy has every right to use his mother's house."

"No, no. First, he's no 'boy'. He's 28 years old, for goodness sake, and Mrs. Clements doesn't want him in the house," Dottie did not pause for any comment from me. "Mrs. Clements never gave him the key and our caretaker, Mr. Brandywine, who has a copy of all our keys, won't make a copy of one for him. So her son, he just climbs in through a back window. He has parties there. Big parties, lots of kids, noisy cars, loud music. Surely you've heard the racket? Your place is less than a mile away."

Dottie's expression indicated that if I hadn't heard the commotion perhaps we ought to have my hearing checked for terminal waxy build up.

"Anyways," she continued without hearing my reaction. "Mrs. Clements has the place completely closed. No water, no electricity, no nothing. That son of hers brings in those big portable booger box radios for music."

"Eventually, what with all that drinking and carrying on, all those party people have to go to the bathroom. But the water is turned off. So do you know what they do when nature calls?"

I dared not guess. I tried to indicate appropriate concern.

Dottie answered her own question, "They go out behind the house and wee wee in the woods."

Then she got to the reason why she walked through the August heat to apprise me of the goings-on of those pesky Clements visitors, "Something has got to be done about that. We want you to do some detecting and put a stop to it."

I was puzzled. Teenagers peeing in the woods did not seem to be the sort of problem to percolate to the top of anyone's "must be stopped" list. After all, as the song said, the birds did it, the bees did it and even educated fleas did it (I think the lyric then suggested, "please do it," but I'm sure it was not referring to pissing in the woods).

I made the mistake of asking, "Why?"

Dottie looked at me as if I were dangerously mad. She straightened so she stood her full 5-foot 2-inches and pinioned me with a stare which assured that I must attend her every word. "If we let them do it," she said, "everyone will want to."

I imagined the senior citizens of Sears Point running amok in the woods, and whizzing with abandon wherever they liked. It was not a pretty picture.

Then Dottie got to the ultimate point, "Jim and I have agreed to hire you to deal with the Clements boy and others of his ilk."

I was about to say that stopping kids from peeing in the woods was hardly an assignment for almost the world's greatest detective, when Uncle Guido sidled up to us, and said, "He'd be glad to help out, Mrs. Gerlund. Who knows some day, perhaps you can return the favor."

I was only upset for a moment until I figured out what Uncle Guido was doing. By helping the Gerlunds maybe we could get on their good side and learn something. After all, how difficult would it be to stop teenagers from whizzing in the woods? Worse comes to worse, I figured all we needed to do was get some neighbors, hold the boy down and apply strategically placed duct tape to seal off any leakage, woodsy or otherwise.

"Sure, I'll pitch in," I said, "and I'll do it for free." Then I cleverly switched their focus of attention. In the detecting game, this was known as doing the unexpected. This allowed me to apply my subtle detecting skills to the more important problem.

"So, Jim," I asked, "Did you ever figure Jerry Andrews needed killing?"

Jim Gerlund sure did look guilty when he stammered, "Well, no. While I would never kill that son of a bibity-bobbity-boo, I'd sure love to go to his funeral."

Then Jim laughed. It was the sort of chortle the Emperor Ming would deliver just after he consigned Flash Gordon to exile with the clay people. It was the laugh of true bad guy and I decided that I should keep an eye on old Jim.

Before I could do any much more of that, George Svaboda nodded his head three times in my direction, either indicating that he wanted to talk to me behind the large mosquito-infested bush growing near the corner of the house or that his forehead had become too heavy for his neck.

I excused myself and walked very slowly towards him. My sex machine was still painfully in neutral – a result of

Amanda drop-kicking my balls -- and I feared some of the tender gears might be stripped if I strode faster.

Without a "by the by" or "how are they hanging," George immediately observed, "Understand you're a detective?"

"Yup," I said. "I'm a gumshoe."

"Personally, I wear leather loafers. I hate gum on my shoes," George said. "No matter, we can still get along. I always say: different strokes make the world go round. OK, so I got a problem. I take care of the Lundgren home, as you know. Every week, the raccoons get into their garbage cans and spread the garbage all over their lawn. Nothing I do-- traps, lights, noise makers, poison--nothing stops them. As a detective, could you take care of this problem for me? They wear masks, so you could think of them as criminals, couldn't you?"

I was suddenly depressed. In the space of a couple of minutes, I was hired to stop teens from pissing in the woods and to keep raccoons out of the garbage.

As I was thinking what Humphrey Bogart as Sam Spade would say, Pro joined the conversation and nudged me in the side. He whispered, "Say yes. It will be good practice. After them, we'd just be moving up the food chain."

So I agreed, "George, I'd be glad to take those raccoons for a long walk off a short pier."

"Oh, no need of that," George said. "Just killing them will be enough."

Uncle Guido squinted at George. Then he said, "You know, if anybody called me a rose bush killer, I'd want to kill him. Roses are so pretty."

I stared at Uncle Guido, not believing that he was actually a fan of roses.

George looked like someone had just told him that he'd won the lottery.

"You are so right. What that Jerry Andrews was saying was unfair. I would never hurt a rose bush. Even when the rose thorns prick me, I tell them I'm sorry for getting close enough to inconvenience them."

It was then that I'd understood that Uncle Guido was getting information by indirection, by going all the way around the barn and coming at the subject after climbing out of the well in the front yard.

So I thought I'd also go at this guy in a roundabout manner. I asked, "So you ever dream of burying Jerry Andrews under his own roses? That would save on fertilizer, wouldn't it?"

My Uncle Guido was looking towards the sky, probably thanking heaven that I was put on this earth.

George protested, "That could either help or hurt the roses, depending on how acidic the body was. What am I saying? I would never want to bury Mr. Andrews anywhere."

He spoke with the wide-eyed innocence of either the completely guilty or the totally innocent. At least that's the way he looked to me.

I quickly interjected, trying to overcome George's suspicions, "Well, we don't even have to think about burying Jerry, who right now is as happy as a fresh frozen chicken."

Uncle Guido gave me a look that indicated I should put a zipper on my mouth. I gave him a small salute indicating that I understood.

By then, the bar-b-cue was pretty much over. Everyone went home, leaving me with several partially eaten chicken carcasses, three new clients, and a growing list of murder suspects.

I sat down with Mr. Jake the Clever Canine. Over the years I have found that I enjoyed talking over the events of the day with good old Mr. Jake. It was a useful exercise that I used it to clear my mind, ponder possibilities and confirm impressions.

As I spoke about Chad, raccoons and woodsy pissers, Mr. Jake turned his back to me and gnawed on a steakbone. Then he farted.

I know that I should not equate dog behavior with humans, but I took that as a canine snub and went right to bed.

Chapter Three

That night I dreamed that I found a bomb.

In the dream, I knew I needed to disarm it, so I opened the metal container that hid the bomb. Inside I found wires labeled "blue wire" and "red wire" and "white wire." Indeed, each wire was the color of the label. I did not know why some mad bomber would stick labels on the wires, but that is what he or she did in my dream.

Within the bomb I also found a clock ticking down the time remaining before it would explode. I knew how much time there was left because this clock had a huge read-out, which could easily be seen from 200 feet away.

Again, I had to ask myself: why did the terrorists in this movie put this enormous electronic clock inside the bomb mechanism? Why put a big, expensive clock inside the bomb where it would (a) never be seen by anyone and (b) would be blown to smithereens when the bomb detonated?

I was frozen in place, not out of fear, but because I was completely stopped while I imagined the conversation between the bomb maker and his terrorist client:

Terrorist: Why put a big clock inside there?

Bomb maker: Do I ask you why you wear funny scarves and shoot rifles into the air?

Terrorist: No, but you could ask that. Wouldn't that clock make the bomb bigger and thus easier to find? And why put it inside when its the only function is to tell the person disarming the bomb how much   time is left, causing him to sweat profusely and possibly earning him an Oscar?

Bomb maker: You are such a nag. All right, if you must know, look at this label. What does it say?

Terrorist: General Electric. But we have nothing against GE.

Bomb maker: When the hero opens the bomb and the audience sees that the clock came from G.E., don't you think we'll be able to get a great discount on a large screen television set?

Terrorist: Ah, that is what we're fighting for.

In the dream I knew that to disarm the bomb I had to cut one wire, but which--the blue, the red or the white. Like most other people who have seen bombs disarmed in movies, I understood that you always, always cut the blue wire.

But, I had to ask myself, did the bomb maker see the same movies I did? Therefore, wouldn't the bomb maker conclude that the blue wire, when cut, should cause the bomb to explode?

In my dream, I was sweating. I did not know what to do.

For some reason, I know that one sure way to disarm the bomb is to dial in a code on a telephone key pad that is beside the electronic clock inside the bomb. Oddly enough, General Electric also built this keypad. In the dream, I happened to know that the correct code was my current girl friend's birthdate, which I had completely forgotten.

I called her on my mobile phone. She answered on the second ring. I asked for her exact birth date. I told her that I was desperate because, if I did not know her birthdate, I could die.

56

She thought for a moment and recalled that I had failed to give her a present the previous year. For some reason this seemed to stir up tremendous antagonism on her part.

She said, "You should remember my birthdate because I told you at the time it was the same day as your mother's birthdate."

After I cried, "So call me bad son, bad son, bad son," she whispered, "Happy death day, sucker" and the phone went dead.

I had to make up my mind in a hurry. I got a power saw and cut the bomb in half. Nothing happened.

Later in my dream, General Electric sent me a $643 bill for destroying one of its key pads and $49 for cutting in half the "Do Not Remove Under Penalty Of Law" tag on the back of the big clock. I learned that, if I had merely cut the clock while leaving the tag intact, there would have been no fine.

That night every light bulb in my apartment went dead. That was when I woke up.

I didn't know what to make of that dream. Was it a foreboding and would it mean that my electricity was about to be cut off? Was it an interpretation of my past and did it mean I should be kind to General Electric in the future? My own interpretation of the dream was that people with chain saws should be forced to get a license.

As I left to start my investigations that morning, I decided that my most lucrative and therefore important case concerned the mysterious reversal of Chad Parkington's opinions a week or so before his disappeared. That was why I went directly to Video Shmideo, the only video store in Saw Mill.

Matt Drudgery, the much-pierced laconic video store clerk, greeted me with as much warmth as he ever put out for any person who wasn't giving him a free burrito, "Hey, Tony, back to rent 'Carhops in Bondage' again?"

That's the problem with being a semi-regular in Sawmill—rent one video for one night to do research into the plight of working women who are forced to wear very small, tight shorts, and I am identified forevermore as a pervert.

Matt continued, "You know, we had that movie for almost three years and you were the only one ever to rent it. Was it good?"

"Matt, my man," I said, "We have the same conversation every time I come in here. It was for research." I sighed wearily to signal that I was mightily tired of this topic.

"Did the 'research' at least have a nice set of jugs?" Matt thought he was very humorous.

To put a stop to his laugh-athon, I demanded, "Do you have a copy of 'Showgirls 2: In Search of Their Lost Virginity'? I need it for a new case I'm working on."

"More 'research'?" Matt rudely asked. "What case is that? A case of blue balls? A case of a date with your own right hand?"

Matt had obviously crossed the line between banter and being an asshole. So I punched him out. Well, actually I only took a swing at him but he defended himself by deftly raising the "Showgirls 2" video box so that it protected his face.

I ended up with badly bruised knuckles while Matt continued his uninterrupted monologue, "What are you calling it? The case of spanking the monkey? The case of the masturbating moron? The case of the dick that peeled his own banana?"

I left with "Showgirls 2" as Matt's braying laughter followed me down the street. Once I got to my parents' home, I settled down with bourbon, branch water and the movie.

I wanted to see what Chad had found interesting or amusing in a film that other critics universally reviled as

"Trash," "Beneath contempt" and "Gives new meaning to the word 'dreck'."

To give Chad some credit, although the script was awful and the acting was worse, I liked the scenes in which Maggie, the stripper with a heart of gold, was befriended by a nice, honest, church-going pimp. To help her out, he located the 10 now-grown-up boys who had taken her virginity on that drunken prom night so many years ago. Then, while Maggie dissolved in tears, the 10 former lovers recreated her loss of virginity so she could remember the night for the rest of her life.

I'm not sure that dressing her in a white garter belt imbued the scene with the proper virginal feeling the director was searching for, but it is possible that Chad might have seen it that way.

The question was: why had Chad liked this film so much?

While searching for an answer, my mind began to clickety-clack off on its own, seemingly without my guidance, which was when I often did my best detecting. As a professional detective, I sometimes merely sit back and observe my own mind in action. It is a finely honed device designed to get to the heart of any case, with only occasional detours into the fervid recesses of my fetid imagination.

For instance, sometimes my mind tries to imagine all the suspects standing naked in a line-up. I have little to do with these thoughts, which can arrive in my mind almost unbidden. However, if I can see the naked suspects in my mind's eye, with folds of fat wallowing over their private parts, they seem less impressive to me and easier to subject to tough questioning. In fact, occasionally I have problems stifling a giggle when I walk up to them and shake their hands.

I must admit that sometimes imagining a female suspect completely nude causes me to lose focus. Then I would have thoughts of spreading Smucker's grape jelly all over her body and I would completely forget the questions I was going to ask. When that happened—and this is a good tip for any aspiring detectives—I knew that I should concentrate harder on the suspect or find a 50-cents-off coupon for Smucker's grape jelly.

At this point, my thinking went as follows: in the detecting business, you either follow the money or the sex. In Chad's case, sex was probably out. Chad was an evil, ugly, angry dwarf and was low on the list of those most likely to add their characteristics to the gene pool.

On one show, one of his partners put out a call for a female evil, ugly, angry dwarf mate for Chad and, as far as I knew, the search had been fruitless. There were absolutely no volunteers from the show's fans for the job of Chad's love mate.

However, Hollywood types might march to the beat of a different sexual tom-tom, I thought. Then I asked myself: what actress, writer or director would want to give up all their self respect in order to seduce an ugly, angry, height-challenged movie critic and thus possibly assure good reviews for the foreseeable future? My immediate answer was: all of them.

My ruminations led me to ask: who would get far more from Chad than he could ever give to her? Only one name came to mind--Freedom Plenty, the talk show host and movie star who combined in her person every possible ethnic minority and dysfunctional family trait.

Freedom was a sometime overweight woman with food issues that caused her to vary from anorexic to binge. She was also a recovering alcoholic drug-abuser, a shopaholic with an abused childhood who was the product of a brief affair between a woman of native American, Japanese, Eskimo and Icelandic heritage and a man who proudly stated he was both white trash and black upwardly mobile. He had abandoned the family when Freedom was only two months old and returned 38 years later to an angry and tear-filled televised reunion. By that time, Freedom had already told her fans that she had given up an illegitimate child when she was a teenager, had endured breast enhancements which were now leaking, had contracted seven different kinds of cancer which were currently in remission, and was also of Polish, Irish, Jewish, and Arab ancestry.

Most recently, on the final show of the season, Freedom had revealed that she suffered from Tourette's syndrome. When Freedom Plenty looked directly at the camera and told everyone at home to "Go fuck yourselves," there was not a dry eye in America and her ratings doubled. Again.

It was rumored that Freedom had dated Chad. The tabloids reported that their apparently stormy relationship was initiated by Freedom because her dating resume was dwarf challenged.

During their courtship, Chad had angered Freedom when he told a reporter that he intended to "cut her down to size." He had also announced, "I'm in this for the money. The woman is rich and I want to be a kept man."

When a reporter asked if Chad would "play the fool," the critic bit the newspaperman on his left calf. The reporter sued Chad for $200 million and the case has yet to be decided.

(Note to self: if Chad is dead and we find a body, no need to go through the effort of finding dental x-rays to prove that the dead person is Chad. All we need to do is match the scar on the left calf of that reporter with Chad's bite.)

After the couple broke up, Freedom went public with her heart-ache and scheduled a week's worth of best-selling authors to counsel her on dealing with the pain. On the last day of the five-part series, Freedom announced that she loved Chad but was ready to move on. The audience gave her a standing ovation. Freedom was one of them and yet she was a survivor.

Almost as soon as that program was broadcast, there was a serious movement to have Freedom declared a saint in the Catholic Church even though Freedom was nominally a Baptist. Her ratings again doubled.

I wondered what if her entire relationship with Chad was merely a way of increasing her popularity? What if she was using the men in her life only to boost ratings? What if America's queen of heartache was a manipulative phony?

The thought was nearly blasphemous, but I found it deliciously enticing nonetheless. If Freedom faked everything, she could actually be harboring resentment against Chad because she feared he would expose her.

Could she have figured out a way to twist his mind so that he would become a movie lover rather than a movie loather? This would lead to the destruction of his show while her popularity was soaring. What sweet revenge that would be.

Then, if my line of reasoning had not wandered off into fallow fields of fluff and fantasy, she might have to kill him for reasons which have more to do with moving this plot along than advancing Freedom's self interest.

Before trying to talk to Freedom, I decided that I needed to check in with Amanda, my beautiful client. She should know what I was planning next.

I fully understood that this was a very dangerous thing to do. I wanted to date her and I even had hopes of becoming involved in a little humpety-hump with her, but I knew that most people who date, befriend or are related to any detective are pursued, terrorized, and often killed by the implacable bad guys.

From my encyclopedic reading of detective novels, I had learned that rule number one of all detectives is: it is always someone close to the detective who dies or is threatened. No relative or friend or helpful witness is ever safe after they become part of the hero's life.

In any Sherlock Holmes story, the murders only begin in earnest after someone goes to Watson and Holmes to ask for protection. Usually, the people Holmes said he would protect are the first to die. It has always seemed to me that the worst move anyone could make was to go to Sherlock Holmes to ask for help.

And that continues today with modern heroes. Being a detective's girlfriend is always just about the most dangerous job in the world.

James Patterson's Lucas Cross had a niece kidnapped and put into a well by one and possibly two serial killers.

Patricia Cornwell's Kay Scarpetta had a niece who often ended up looking at the wrong end of guns and knives held by madmen.

John Sandford's detective Lucas Davenport dated a Finnish doctor who always had near-death experiences whenever she was near Davenport. Crazed murderers put guns to her head and serial killers stalked her.

Sometimes the loved one is safe only because they're going to die anyway. Ridley Pearson's detective Lou Boldt's wife, Elizabeth, has been staying out of the crosshairs of the crazed killers only because she has been battling lymphoma for several books.

So the question was:

Should I reveal the depth of my passion to Amanda and begin a serious relationship with her? Would that put her life in jeopardy? Just how ethical should I be on this issue?

Should I warn Amanda that any impending close and loving relationship with me might result in her being kidnapped, shot, stabbed and/or dismembered by a serial killer?

I decided to keep my mouth shut. Warning Amanda violated the moral bedrock of my personal universe, which is: let nothing stand between me and the possible nooky. Dating me was a chance she would just have to take.

Returning to my parents' home, I recalled how my last conversation with Amanda had ended. I prepared myself for my next encounter with her by putting an iron skillet down the front of my pants.

My motto is: kick me in the balls once and you hurt me. Kick me in the balls twice and you hurt yourself.

Amanda answered the door wearing a long, slinky sheer black nightgown slit up to her hips. Her apparel caused an instant reaction. The iron skillet in my pants began ringing as if a gong were being hit by a mallet.

She asked, "What is that odd sound?"

"What sound?" I nervously asked while my pants again went kraaannng!

Trying to get her mind off the sound, I proudly announced, "Amanda, I'd like to report on my investigation."

"You came fast."

"Actually, I won't come for at least another four seconds if I can just remember the guy who played second base for the Cubs in 1967 and..."

Then I stopped myself and laughed when I realized she was referring to my arrival on her doorstep. Amanda beckoned me to enter. As I did, she observed, "Is that a skillet in your pants or are you happy to see me?"

"Both," I said as nonchalantly as anyone could whose raging erection was playing "The Anvil Chorus" in his pants. "I have just two questions. First, would you mind if I talked to Freedom Plenty to see if she had anything to do with Chad's change of heart?"

"Sure. Why not?"

Amanda seemed to be in a most agreeable mood, so I quickly brought up my second, and most important, question. I decided to phrase my request as a jovial, light, insouciant suggestion, even thought I'm not sure what insouciant meant.

64

Smiling, holding my arms open and apart from my body, speaking in a confident and confidential tone while attempting to make sure that Amanda felt as comfortable and as un-threatened as possible, I asked, "Would you like to go out with me? A date would sure be a lot more fun that suing you for assault and sexual harassment."

"Assault and sexual harassment!?" Amanda seemed miffed and mystified.

I explained, "According to my reading of the law, you're my boss—at least for this case--and you punted my privates the last time we met."

You know, even with the protection of the iron skillet, when you get kicked in the balls, it still tingles. In Amanda's living room, it sounded like the beginning of one of those old J. Arthur Rank movie productions when a huge, strong, sweating man wearing a diaper would hit a large gong. Amanda was obviously a person who kicked first and asked questions later.

I gasped, "I assume that means no?"

"It means yes. I may be angry," Amanda said, "but I'm no fool. In this age of political correctness, you'd probably win a sex harassment suit against me. Sure I'll go out with you. I may even have sex with you as soon as you figure out what's happened to Chad."

Putting on my most debonair look, winking at her in a co-conspiratorial manner, and attempting to imitate the Brad Pitt cat who swallowed the Catherine Zeta-Jones mouse, I asked, "But will you blow me?"

You know, a second kick in the skillet hurt almost as much as the first time. It was not something I would ever get used to. In any case, neither kick to the skillet was as painful as Amanda's first assault on my unprotected family jewels, for which I was grateful.

Since Amanda had clearly given me permission to question Freedom Plenty about Chad's disappearance, I decided to walk (or rather limp) over to the Plenty mansion.

A good detective never really walks. He saunters, moving his shoulders in a tough-guy rhythm while constantly sizing up the situation as if he had eyes hanging out on long stalks to see behind him and around corners.

I was sauntering over to Freedom Plenty's estate when I smelled him before I saw him. The guy carried with him the aroma of cheap aftershave lotion of the sort that's advertised to make you smell like a jaunty sailor but which actually imparts the fragrance of overflowing toilets below decks.

My sensitive nostrils also picked up the odor of bourbon aged in plastic, of fear seeped in bile and the faintest whiff of the balsam they put in cheap shampoos that you get for free in sleazy hotels that do not charge for the extra bedbugs. As you can tell, I have a sensitive nose.

I didn't have to wait long. He sidled up to me, an easy move since I was only sauntering.

I could tell from the bulge in his jacket that he was packing heat. Judging by the outline the weapon made, I knew he had a Rutger Hauer Sig Sauer .92 caliber, a serious weapon commonly known as the Subway Deflowerer, with 13 bullets in the chamber and 27 more in the grip. It was the same pistol that Clint Eastwood used to shoot through a refrigerator and two feet of concrete in that great film "The Dry, The Sere and the Hacking."

The stranger dogging my steps and panting in my ear was a pasty face dude, wiry in an untrustworthy way, with a mean sneer plastered on his nondescript face. He had the eyes of a snake in the grass that's about to swallow a baby mouse that's just beginning to enjoy life but will never smell its mother's breasts again.

"Pssst," he hissed, "Wanna buy the Watchtower?"

"Aren't you guys supposed to pass that out for free along with advice about God's path?" I asked. "Aren't you supposed to bore me on Sunday afternoons just as the football game is starting? What is a guy like you doing selling the Watchtower?"

"Getting your attention," he said, "But I think I need to be a little more persuasive."

The sucker punch came out of nowhere and hit me in the side of the head. For the first time in my short career as a detective, I could hear the little birdies tweeting. They resembled the birds that fly around Daffy Duck's head after he's slugged by Elmer Fudd and the song they were singing was, "Lie down and be quiet, you'll feel better."

The pasty-face dude said, "Don't go sticking your nose where it don't belong."

"What the hell does that mean?" I asked as I got to my feet. "If you're talking about that high school girl a few years ago, we were the same age at the time, we never did have sex, and she wanted my nose right where I put it."

"Look," he growled, "I'm just a messenger. Listen to the message."

I observed, "If this is about that job shooting raccoons, I don't have to, I don't want to, I don't need to shoot raccoons. I love raccoons. Some of my best friends are..."

My attacker seemed to be getting angrier by the second. He shouted, "This has nothing to do with any God damned raccoons. Shoot every friggin' raccoon in the forest for all I care. Listen, just keep your nose clean and..."

There was no reasoning with the man, but I tried. I said, "Of course I keep my nose clean. Why the hell do you think I constantly pick it, especially when I'm driving and..."

The guy hit me in the stomach. Hard.

As I doubled over, wheezing, he cursed to himself, "It's like talking to some fuckin' demented Bugs Bunny."

The pasty face dude seemed to get very tired about then. He said, "Look, it makes no never-mind to me if you cooperate and live to a ripe old age or you don't go-along-to-get-along and I cut you up in little bits and feed you to a feral pack of unemployed dot com secretaries."

But I yelled right back at him, "I know what's going on. I saw the sequel to 'Silence of the Lambs.' Been there, done that, my gourmand friend. If you want to eat gray matter, eat your own brains. My brain wouldn't help a bird. So, go ahead: try to say something real scary to me."

He said it, "Don't be a buddinsky. The world hates buddinskys."

But I was faster than he was. I pointed to the sky and sang, "Look up. Look down. Don't frown."

That was when I brought the edge of my hand under his nose, collecting a small amount of dripping snot on my little finger but delivering a fair amount of pain with a knife edge thwack to his proboscis.

I said, "One sucker punch deserves another," and walked off.

As I left, I heard him speak with disturbing nasality, "Don't stick you nose in other people's business. You could lose your nose and then you'd look even worse than you do now."

I was pleased about my meeting with the punching Watchtower salesman because it was almost exactly what would have happened to Raymond Chandler's star detective. Philip Marlowe could sit next to someone in a bar and, before you could whistle the chorus to "Old Macdonald Had a Farm," without the animal imitations, just about everyone within shouting distance would be beating him up and warning him to stay away from things he didn't much care about in the first place.

My sucker punching attacker's warning meant that my investigations were getting somewhere, but I hadn't the foggiest idea where. It meant that I was stepping on the right toes. But I had to ask myself: whose toes? And if they were touchy about their toes, would they next step on my balls?

Of all the stuff I was investigating, what was most likely to result in a sucker punch upside my head? My mind swept across my client list like a search light without a surge protector.

Merry Martha had an angry husband, but I didn't think he knew that Martha and I were playing the two-humped camel at the oasis of depravity.

Stopping kids from pissing in the woods shouldn't bring on that kind of heat. First because I hadn't done anything about that yet. And second, it would only result in that level of threat if those kids really, really needed to keep pissing in the woods.

Figuring out why Chad loved movies just before he disappeared shouldn't bring any heat on me and probably not even on him. A reviewer that loves everything suddenly has lots of friends.

So, by a process of deduction it came down to the stiff getting stiffer in my parents' freezer. That's when it occurred to my fine detective's mind that maybe the guy who had killed Jerry Andrews wanted the body found, was disappointed that there was no murder investigation, and had sent the pasty-faced goon to threaten me so I'd unload my freezer immediately, if not sooner.

That led to more questions: why had Jerry been murdered in my parents' home? Did the murder have something to do with dad? Or mom? Or me? Or Uncle Guido?

I had to admit that I have absolutely no answer to the following question: why hadn't I asked these questions a lot earlier? So I continued asking myself other questions.

Did the murder have anything to do with Jerry's well known sexual successes? Or was he killed because of a decision he made as president of the association? Was it maybe just sloppiness, an incident in which someone murdered Jerry and then accidentally put the body in our living room rather than in the dump?

I was also struck by the thought that perhaps I had too much stuff on my plate. I figured the way to start cleaning off my dish with the scrub brush of determination was by going ahead with my investigation of Chad and his fascinating relationship with Freedom Plenty.

One of Freedom Plenty's homes was an Indiana farm slightly larger than Maine. She was helicoptered to it every day, moments after the taping of her show.

She was, as far as I was concerned, one of the bravest and most wonderful women I had ever heard about. Her battles with her own waistline was take-no-prisoners monumental, and each diet had been chronicled on her TV show, in her magazine and on her web site.

Over the years, Freedom Plenty had gained and lost the weight of the entire Chicago Bears 1986 Super Bowl defensive unit. Her girth has ranged from a size 3 to a size 40, with many stops in-between.

But that is not all. Her battles against stalkers, rapers, a poor self image (the biggest foe of all) and a hundred other modern crosses-to-bear have become the stuff of countless television and radio shows, books and made-for-television movies.

As I walked down the long, tree-shaded lane that led to her columned mansion, I could see her many likenesses frozen for all time in the statuary that lined the driveway. There was the sylph-like Freedom of June,1994, after a well-publicized diet allowed her to lose 74.3 pounds in just three weeks through a combination of frequent exercise and constant vomiting.

Who can forget her entrance at the beginning of the TV season after she had lost the weight? Freedom was wearing a small sequined bra and tight silk pants, which revealed no outline of any panties or panty hose. She walked through the wildly applauding audience, jumped on the stage and turned around three times to show everyone the new, less plentiful Freedom Plenty and received a standing ovation.

70

Beside her on the stage on which she made her grand entrance that afternoon was a huge, dripping, flowing, oozing pile of plastic fat--a representation of the exact amount of fat Freedom had lost after having her stomach stapled 27 times (the staples later came loose, traveled through her bowels and resulted in a prize-winning five-part series titled "Staple Me Not"). It was her triumphant night.

But the defeat of what she called "her demon fat" was quickly followed by binge eating (first chronicled in the tabloids under the headline "Freedom Knows No Boundaries"). Within three months, all the weight she had lost was re-gained...and more.

When Freedom was 155 pounds heavier than she was on the night the big weight loss was revealed to the world, she commissioned yet another statue. That was displayed beside the skinny Freedom and it was a bloated image worthy of a depressed Rubens in a bitter funk.

Freedom's haunches in the statue were monumental, her ass was unfettered and enormous, and rolls of fat draped her knees and dribbled over her hips.

According to the plaques on the other statues lining the walk, only six months later Freedom once again became thin enough to replace Ally McBeal as the anorexia poster girl. The next statue, completed three months later and standing beside the skinny Freedom, again revealed her in a sumo-wrestling mode.

All the statues were nudes. Freedom hid nothing from her audience as this sculpture walk proclaimed. Her breasts achieved earth-mother status for one statue and dwindled to microscopic pips for the next. Her posterior ballooned to alarming (and yet compelling) proportions in one statue, only to disappear like a runway model's appetite in the next.

In each of the statues, I could see Freedom Plenty's need to please her fans and herself. This lane of weight-shifting images was an overwhelming projection of personal vulnerability. And it affected me deeply.

I must have entered some sort of emotional swoon akin to what I think they call "sartorial," the eastern projection into the nether worldly ideal only available to Japanese sushi chefs with runaway ginsu knives.

Rather than proceed immediately to the house, ring the bell, and demand an audience with the people's queen, something made me stop at one of the more magnificent statues of the well-padded Ms. Plenty.

Seemingly without any volition on my part, my hand slowly reached out and began stroking her beautiful, bounteous, sensuous, sculptural butt.

As my head rested between her cold metallic cheeks, I gave myself over to the feeling of deep involvement in Freedom's plight, her quest, her ideals and the feeling that this metal monument was the most perfect ass I had ever known.

At the precise moment of my deepest reverie when my most intimate, spiritual connection with Freedom's womanliness was at its peak, I was interrupted by a single, loudly-demanded question, "What the hell are you doing?"

My head snapped back as I instantly returned to my senses. I did not stammer, I did not stutter. Despite my momentary confusion, I was able to rely on the confidence I had learned after surviving many embarrassing situations. I quickly answered, "Nothing."

"Oh yah?" my interrupter sneered. "You expect me to believe you were doing 'nothing' when it looked to me like you were whispering into that statue's ass. Is that right? Are you a member of the ass whisperers, who have threatened to invade us so often? Were you plotting against us? Are you preparing to murder and maim me right now? I can feel you thinking bad thoughts about me."

"Why, that's absurd," I said. "Completely Bat-zoid."

"A-ha, you think I'm crazy? No, I'm not and I'll prove it to you. Take one step towards me and I'll stab myself 54 times and any pain I suffer will be your fault."

72

My questioner was a skinny, nervous guy with fingernails chewed to the quick. He was a collection of herky-jerky movements so frantic that all by himself he made a mosh pit look like a sea of serenity.

"Who are you?" I asked.

"Wouldn't you like to know?" he replied. "All of you would, then you could take over my body the way you've taken over my mind by frying my brain with laser beams from the Planet Corpulent."

I had heard the stories that Freedom was guarded by an army of her most devoted fans, volunteers who had not made much psychological progress in combating the personality disorders that took them to the Freedom Plenty show in the first place. They loved her so much that they gave up their lives just to be near her.

It was said that Freedom's army, which she fed and clothed, essentially functioned on the level of a herd of geese. They couldn't really do much except make a lot of noise, but they could do that rather well, as my interrogator proved.

Almost all of Freedom's Dysfunctional Army (FDA) had trouble with authority figures. They routinely disobeyed sergeants, lieutenants, captains, etc. At the same time, most FDA volunteers believed that only God could tell them what to do. When given an order by someone who was not God, the average FDA member would stand perfectly still awaiting word from Higher Authority. This made any organized activity rather difficult.

My interrogator was obviously with the FDA. I was certain of that when he interrupted his conversation with me to quiz himself using two voices. One was high-pitched, whining and nagging while the other was low, authoritative and insistent.

As he spoke, he swung his head back and forth. After emphasizing particularly insulting words, he would slap himself on the forehead or across his face.

He yelled: "Who are you?"

Then he'd answer himself, "What business is it of yours?"

Quickly he'd screech, "Don't give me that lip."

Then the back and forth, "A little respect, young man."

"That's just what I give you, a very little respect, you bed-wetting momma's boy."

"Just shut your pie hole."

At that point, my self-interrogator picked up a stick and attempted to bash himself in the head with it. Fortunately, his left hand quickly grabbed his right hand and the FDA fell to the ground, wrestling with himself.

I heard him crying and yelling, "Mother loved you more."

"Not true, a million times not true."

"Oh, yes she did, did, did."

"Did not."

In seconds, the poor man was reduced to swearing, swatting and kicking himself.

Since my appearance was the cause of his distress, I decided to leave him alone and proceed to the mansion's massive front doors. These seemed to be made of lead and were tall enough to allow an Apollo rocket to pass through.

A tasteful bas relief sculpture was embedded in the doors and it depicted Freedom Plenty dressed as a Medieval knight slaying a dragon labeled "ratings" and a sinuous snake called "macho-man."

A huge man wearing what appeared to be equal parts of a general's uniform and a scullery maid's dress immediately blocked my path into the house. He said, "I suppose you want to get in to see Freedom Plenty like everyone else in the known universe."

"I have an appointment," I said as calmly as I could, though my previous encounter with the guard who interrogated himself had left me shaken.

"Sure, sure," he sneered. "That's what they all say. Before you see her you have to fill out this security form, and all your answers better be truthful. We have ways of getting the truth out of everyone. Ev-ry-wan."

"What form?"

"The one I'm holding in my hand."

"I don't see any form."

"Good, you passed the first test. Congratulations, you are in touch with reality."

I asked, "How many people have actually flunked that so-called test?"

"That's top secret, need to know," he announced. "In other words, it's for me to know and for you never to find out. Moving right along: test number two: what's my name?"

"I don't know," I said with some testiness.

"That's actually my middle name," he said, proudly. "I was born during an Abbott and Costello 'Who's on First?' routine. You get extra credit for that answer and, because you were so good with the first two questions, you do not have to answer questions three through 345. The final test: prove that you love Freedom Plenty and that you add to the world's supply of human dysfunctions. Oh, never mind the first. We know you love her."

"How do you know that?" I queried.

"News of that kiss you planted on her statue's ass preceded you," he said. "You are the first person ever to do something like that."

I insisted, "I was only resting."

"Sure, sure," he said, "And Rip Van Winkle was only napping. Do you have any known dysfunctions?"

I thought about that for a while and finally came up with one, "My socks never match. It's not completely the laundry's fault. I believe that the sock manufacturers have secretly added some compound to my socks so that late at night they molt and change into mismatched pairs."

"That'll do. Congratulations, no other sock-challenged personality has ever met Freedom Plenty. I envy you." With that, he smiled and opened the door, and I was finally able to enter her private sanctum.

She was reclining on a chaise lounge in a simply furnished living room, which was in keeping with the lack of pretension that she communicated on her daily television program. The furnishings were early dormitory room, with an imitation Formica white desk, couches covered with a plaid material that could be found an any resale shop in the country, and a variety of wicker chairs that seemed to have been purchased at garage sales.

The only outward indication that Freedom Plenty was worth over half a billion dollars was in the size of the room. The Cathedral of Notre Dame could have easily fitted in here with a couple of football fields left over for nunneries.

Freedom, I am pleased to report to her millions of fans, was in one of her thinnish phases. She appeared to be less than blimp size but more than central African famine victim, which has so clearly become the current ideal for the average American female.

As a matter of fact, I can honestly report that she looked quite sexy in a see-through, tan caftan that was slit well above her left buttock. The way the material of her dress was tossed casually to one side revealed all her upper thigh and most of her haunch. Once again I could feel a swoon coming on and I had to resist the intense, dizzying desire to rest my cheek on any one of hers.

I also have the responsibility to her fans to reveal that she was in a good mood, upbeat and pleasant -- at least a 9.5 out of 10 on the PMS --the Plenty Mood Scale. Several major daily newspapers offer daily charts on Freedom's moods, along with horoscopes, advice to lovelorn and tips on refinishing furniture.

Some of her fans have protested the subjective nature of these charts, which are compiled after rigorous analyses of Freedom's many public appearances by a panel of seven distinguished psychiatrists.

As is often the case with any new idea, it became controversial. A rival paper, which did not carry the Plenty Mood Scale, investigated the panel responsible for it and discovered that all of its members had written self-help books. The implication was that the sales of these books would benefit enormously if the authors were asked to appear as guests on the Freedom Plenty program.

It was said that the psychiatric panel, like stock market analysts, shaded their reports on Freedom's moods and made them more positive than they deserved to be. That way, Freedom would enjoy reading her charts and would be friendlier to the publicists for the psychiatric panel when they asked about appearances on her program.

Noelle Spangler, Freedom's spokes person, vigorously denied any such collusion and threatened law suits against anyone who "Even thought such thoughts."

That created an even bigger controversy until Freedom took several minutes at the beginning of her TV program to deny that she had ever considered suing to prevent the thoughts of any psychiatrist or investigative journalist. She was instantly and completely believed.

Every panelist responsible for the PMS scale subsequently appeared on Freedom's shows and each one of them offered a little joke about the contretemps. The best line was spoken by Dr. Hans Munchkin, author of "Relationship Potching: Spank Your Way to a Fulfilling Marriage," who said, "If you buy my book because Freedom is in a good mood, you're a crazy nutcase and I'll turn you over my powerful thighs and personally tan your naked butt."

At last report, Dr. Munchkin was having some difficulty making good on his threat because carpal tunnel syndrome had affected his right (or spanking) hand.

At the start of our conversation, by way of greeting, Freedom cocked a well-practiced eyebrow in my direction and said with great sincerity, "Thank you, Mr. Testa. No one has ever kissed my statue's ass before."

I was about to protest that I was only resting my head when Freedom said, "As a kid, I always wanted to be a detective."

The woman was amazing--she could find something in common with anyone in the world. I asked, "Was it just a kid's fantasy?"

"Oh, no," she enthused. "When I was 16 years old, I began following people to see where they went. I figured that way I could learn what it was like being a detective. I followed my friends, guys that I wanted to be my boyfriends, relatives, people in the neighborhood. Today I guess it would be called 'stalking' but I thought I was studying to be a detective. It was fascinating. I followed my brother and learned that he was gay. I followed my dad and discovered that he was a part-time pimp with a stable of four working girls. But enough about my not-so innocent past. How can I help you?"

My first thought was about the millions of people who yearned to have her ask that question of them.

My second thought was that there should be some way to make some additional money out of her revelations, but I rejected that. I was there to help discover why Chad had changed his reviewing style and then vanished. After that, I had plenty of time to notify the National Enquirer about anything we said to each other.

I said, "You dated Chad Parkington?"

"We went out," Freedom whispered. "But we seldom saw eye to eye."

78

I asked, "Had you recently noticed anything different about Chad?"

"No, by now I can pretty much overlook him," Freedom said. "But I did enjoy dancing with him. You do know that his head only came up to there," indicating her waist, "Dancing cheek to crotch with him was one of the dreamiest experiences of my life."

"I'll bet," I enthusiastically agreed, even though I wasn't exactly sure what she was talking about.

"Speaking of dreamy moments," I added, attempting to create the smoothest of transitions, "Chad seems to like every movie he sees these days. Do you have any notion why he's had this sudden change of heart on the Three Guys TV show?"

"Somebody could have put him up to it," Freedom said.

"Why did you break up with him?" I asked, hopefully cutting to the heart of the matter.

"Because he didn't measure up."

"Please be specific. Was it his personality?"

"Yes," Freedom said. "Chad was small-minded."

I should have been appalled by her rapid-fire, off-hand, politically incorrect jokes, making fun of the height-challenged Chad. After all, Chad was both a midget and a client. But I wasn't upset until it occurred to me that Freedom might also make jokes about me after I left.

I inquired, "Did you and Chad ever have sex?"

"Why do you want to know?"

Isn't it interesting that people who make their living asking embarrassing, pointed questions of others almost never enjoy answering embarrassing, pointed questions themselves.

My Uncle Guido often reminded me, "On quiz shows and in life, it's better to ask the questions than answer them." With that in mind, I answered, "Just call me an insatiably curious gossip monger, a keyhole peeper into the lives of people better and more important than me, and a slimy skulking sleeze-ball who ferrets out secrets for resale to a low-class public."

"Good," she said, happily. "I'm happy to talk to an honest man. The answer is yes, we did make love, but he came up short."

At this point, I thought of suggesting that experiencing my full enchilada might be just the transcending experience she needed, but I decided to tantalize her rather than jumping in like a bull looking for the washroom in a Mexican restaurant.

So I shifted in my chair and adjusted my balls to allow them to rest more comfortably in my pants. The indirect approach is often the best, especially when I was hoping for another invitation from her.

Sensing that she was almost out of short guy jokes, I knew I needed to wrap up our discussion. However, never for a moment did I forget my promise to Amanda to avoid at all costs mentioning the words "Disappeared" and "Chad" in the same sentence. So I asked, "How would you feel if Chad vamoosed into thin air?"

"I'd be a little upset," she admitted, "But I'd also look under all the beds. He was a little guy and he could hide in the darnedest places. I found him nude, curled up in my underwear drawer one night."

I wished she hadn't told me that. Even as a detective, it was more information than I wanted or needed. It would take me a long time to rid my mind of tiny Chad curled up in Freedom's skivvies. I asked, "Can you think of anyone else I should talk to you about matter?"

Freedom was quick to respond, "Since I'm not sure what we've been talking about other than sex with midgets, you probably ought to talk to Don D'Wangle, Chad's agent.

He also represents me. In fact, Don introduced us and suggested that a few dates would help both our careers."

Striving for the perfect sense of sisterhood with her, I observed, "So he thought it would be good for you to get laid by a runt?"

"Chad hated just two words: runt and diminutive," she revealed.

"Whatever yanked his chain," I said. "But what would be the advantage for the teeny-tiny Chad-ster in dating a full-sized woman such as yourself?"

"Oh, Mr. Testa," she purred. "I fear that Chad always loved to bite off more than he could ever chew."

She then graced me with the most fetching, secretive smile, indicating that Freedom and Chad enjoyed intimate experiences only available to certain barnyard animals. No matter how hard I tried, I had difficulty imagining that.

Freedom continued, "But be careful, Mr. Testa. D'Wangle has been known to sign up almost everyone he meets and get 10 per cent of his or her earnings. I hear he's got representation contracts with his marriage counselor, his garbage collector and his masseuse. No private dicks in his mix. Watch out or you end up with an agent you may or may not want."

As I walked away from Freedom's redoubt, I was struck by the certainty that I was getting nowhere fast, walking down the blind alleys of remembrance into the cul-de-sacs of ignorance, as my third grade teacher would say just before taking me into the cloak room and tanning my naked bottom with a rug beater. But that is another story to be told later for an even more lucrative book contract.

I didn't want Freedom to be a suspect because I wanted to help her, as did everyone else on earth. And I had the advantage of actually talking to her.

Note to self: Next time, seduce Freedom because that would be of great comfort to her. If you do not offer her the opportunity to experience your love missile, then ask for her autograph.

Idea as addendum to note to self: what if I could get her to sign my private parts? Would I ever want to bathe again?

Second idea as second addendum to note to self: carry indelible ink pen with you at all times just in case Freedom agrees request for full body signature.

Fifth or sixth note to self: Ask someone with medical knowledge: would it be too painful then to sell that signature? Can a skin transplant cover the affected area once the old skin has been sold?

Come to think of it, perhaps it would work out for the best if I always carried a simple autograph book.

As I walked back to my parents' weekend home, I ruminated on the cases I had. Any detective would do that because going over as-yet unsolved cases would stall the plot, allow the reader to catch up and add to the number of pages in the book so the publisher could charge more money per copy.

I figured I had thought so much about Chad that I was getting a headache. My forehead was throbbing with the jungle drums of migraine. So I turned my thoughts to the dead body I found in my parents' living room.

Jerry Andrews' death and the fact that his body was still in my parents' freezer could mean jail or execution or worse for me. (At that moment, I could not imagine "worse" and didn't want to try.)

Note to self: is it possible that mom or dad murdered Jerry? Check this out. Also, could I simply put the blame on them and settle this whole mess?

When I got back to my parents' home, I found Uncle Guido and Pro having a cup of coffee in the kitchen. Uncle Guido was advising Pro, "When giving criticism to your subordinates, never punch both the guy's ears at once. How's he going to hear what you have to say after that?"

And there I was, once again, without a notebook when I needed one in order to save Uncle Guido's wisdom for all eternity.

The two men were exhausted. They told me that they knew going in that Merry Martha had no interest in finding her lost salami.

Uncle Guido said, "The salami thing was only a ruse to get us over there. I told her I knew what her problem was. It was that Michael Douglas thing, what do you call it? Oh, yah, she's a nitro-maniac, also known as a sex-aholic. That is someone who wants it all the time."

"According to that definition," I offered, "Aren't we all basically sexaholics?"

"To a degree," Uncle Guido wisely observed.

Pro said that Martha asked them if there was any cure and they both agreed to give her, ahem, therapy. The session took the entire night and they didn't think they had cured her.

Uncle Guido added, "We had to get out of there while we could walk on our own steam."

Uncle Guido then asked, "Her dog was locked out on the porch all night barking. You'd think the neighbors would complain." I said nothing at that point.

Uncle Guido and Pro had also been discussing who might have killed Jerry Andrews. They both believed that the murder was a message to them. A message? Obviously, these guys deal with people who have never heard of Western Union, the telephone or email.

Uncle Guido voted for, "No Nose Noogosa. The son of a bitch hates me."

But Pro said, "Doing 3 to 10 in Stateville. No Nose ain't stickin' his nose in other people's business no more, unless it's his prison girlfriend's."

"Then how about 'The Carrot' Koslowski? He said he'd have me killed."

Pro shook his head, "The Carrot is stewed--died last year. Maybe root rot got him?"

"We should be so lucky," Uncle Guido laughed. "What about 'Taps' Sinclair? He said he wanted to kill everyone in my family."

Pro very patiently explained, "That's why we took care of Taps. He's now resting in the northbound exit from the Kennedy Expressway at Lawrence Avenue. Remember? You even said we should play 'Taps' for Taps."

Uncle Guido shook his head and smiled at the memory.

"Why northbound?" I asked.

Pro patiently explained that the southbound ramp was already occupied by several other close associates, including "Gumbo" Spumoni, "Trembles" Cacciatore, "Viagra" Genviana, "Suspension" Balduceri and others.

Because it was something I had always found curious, I asked them how guys in the outfit got their nicknames and why all their names were Italian.

Uncle Guido explained that years ago, after a discrimination complaint from the Justice Department, the outfit was forced to open its ranks. "Our thing," as Uncle Guido sometimes referred to organized crime now included people from all cultures, religions and nationalities: Swedes, Jews (who had always been in the outfit), African Americans, Native Americans, French, English, Germans, a Hottentot or two, and so on.

The nicknames, Uncle Guido patiently explained, were based on that old story of the native American lad who asked his father if it is true that Indian children are named after the first thing the baby sees after they are born. According to legend, the father responded, "Why do you ask, Two Dogs Fucking?"

Pro said, "A guy does something or has some characteristic and that gives him a nickname. Once the newspaper reporters would give the nicknames to us, but there were complaints. Guys didn't enjoy being called 'Needle Dick' or 'Squats.' It could even be harmful to your health if the news guys nicknamed you 'Squealer' or 'Big Mouth.' So now, when you join the organization, you are given a nickname during our solemn naming ceremony. That way we can pre-empt the creeps in the media and come up with our own nomenclature."

Uncle Guido continued, "During that same ceremony, the new person is given their official Italian last name, just to continue the tradition. 'Gumbo' Bonavennia was originally Stanley Dumpfbrunner, a German kid."

I asked, "If I joined your organization, what would my name be?"

Uncle Guido thought for a few moments. Then he smiled and said, "That's easy. We'd call you Two Dogs Fucking."

Uncle Guido and Pro enjoyed that joke much more than I did.

Then Uncle Guido got very serious. He looked me right in the eye and said, "There's Someone You Should Talk To."

I asked, "What is his name?"

Uncle Guido looked both ways before answering, "That's his name. Over the years, this guy has been referred to as Someone You Should Talk To so often that he legally changed his name."

I was confused, "What do I call him?"

Pro, who seemed a little impatient with me, interjected, "You don't call him nothing. He's Someone You Should Talk To."

I asked, "What do I call him for short? Does he have a nickname?"

Pro advised, "Don't go tying your balls in no friggin' half-hitch, bowline cinch knot. Listen with both ears, OK? You are going to see Someone You Should Talk To. Kapeesh?"

I understood. And I shut up, even though I wanted to ask Uncle Guido what the guy's mother called him when she was on the telephone complaining that her back pains were making it difficult to pee. I wanted to know what his girlfriend called him when she was about to have the fireworks of ecstasy erupt and what his best buddy called him when he was being teased about not getting laid as frequently as he did in his twenties. But I knew I would wait until the right time to ask these questions.

So we drove into Chicago and went over to the pizza joint that was his headquarters. Uncle Guido handled the introductions, "Tony, I want you to meet Someone You Should Talk To."

"Please to meet you," I said. "Can I call you just Someone or Some for short?"

Uncle Guido looked to heaven for some relief, Pro began reaching for his pistol and Someone You Should Talk To turned red in the face.

Someone You Should Talk To whispered, "Are we talking or fooling around?"

"Talking," I said. "I don't fool around with guys."

"Good," he said. "Guido here wants my opinion about the 'inconvenience' that was in your folks' living room the other night. I told him what I'm telling you. It was definitely a message.

Then it was my turn to get upset, "A message? Don't you guys ever use phones?"

"Phones can be tapped." Someone You Should Talk To spoke so calmly and softly that I could hardly hear him.

I added, "I mean, shit, there's Western Union."

"Anyone can read a telegram."

86

"What about using the U. S. Mails? That's what they're there for!"

"You want we should put it in writing, huh? Maybe inside a Hallmark Card? Something like 'To my former business associate: loved working with you when you were alive, like it better now that you are soon to be dead.' Tony, to put it into words even you might understand, our business model is not compatible with the U. S. Anything, let alone mail."

"What about email?"

"We never expose our communications to hackers. If there's any hacking to be done, we do it ourselves."

The argument was rapidly going around in circles the way a dog that needs to pee does a series of 360's on a marble cocktail table that's also advertising lite beer. So I tried a different tactic. I asked, "So who would send that message?"

"Could be anyone," said Someone You Should Talk To. "Cops could do it if they were feeling frisky."

"Frisky?" I interjected in disbelief. "A frisky cop would shoot a nearly naked man and dump the body in my parents' home as a way of telling my uncle something?"

I was beginning to think I was at a murderous Mad Hatter's tea party.

"Definitely frisky," Someone You Should Talk To insisted. "Or it could be an associate of Guido, or one of his enemies, or someone who happened to pass Guido in the street and didn't like the cut of his jib."

He continued, "Or it could be someone Guido never knew who wanted to tell Guido something. Or the perpetrator could want Guido to tell someone else something and the body was the means of delivering the message."

"In other words," I said, a little exasperated, "It could be anyone and everyone."

"Right," said Someone You Should Talk To. "Anyone except you, me and Guido, and, frankly, I'm a little suspicious about both of you."

After our exceedingly frustrating conversation, I was struck by the fact that the list of possible suspects seemed to be growing faster than a politician's hard on when presented with the possibility of a lucrative bribe for voting the way he would have voted without the monetary incentive.

Not that I was surprised. That was pretty much the way it was whenever a detective entered the picture in any story about gumshoes. Even Sherlock Holmes would spend the entire story moping around, talking to all sorts of people and, in the end, everyone remained as much under suspicion as they were when the effort started.

When I originally found the body, it seemed that Jerry's enemies in Saw Mill might have wanted him eliminated and that would have added up to about a dozen people (I have taken my name off the suspects list because, after all, it is my list and I can have on it whomever I want.)

Jealous husbands and jilted wives caused that list to swell, but that was nothing compared with the added suspects brought into the picture by Someone You Should Talk To. If we accepted his reasoning, the suspects list now included all the 4 billion human beings on this planet plus any aliens pissed off at Jerry Andrews because the Little Green Men didn't appreciate Jerry balling their Big Green Wives.

Chapter Four

The next morning, Uncle Guido announced, "I got to do some checking on my own to learn what the street is saying."

I figured the elderly have their strange ways and, if Uncle Guido wanted to be seen in public talking to curbs and center dividing lines, he could do so without me. So I cheerily said, "Wish them good drainage for me."

Uncle Guido and Pro looked a little mystified when I went off on my own investigations, having remembered that I owed a visit to some of my potential clients. I soon found myself standing in front of the Gerlund's home at the top of King's Roost, the paved-over dune that overlooked Sears Point.

Jim had an easy manner and an amiable smile befitting someone who was the former president of the homeowner's association. Around Sears Point, he was known as "A Card." Before visiting him in his home, I could never figure out why. Now I know.

They invited me to sit in their knotty-pine paneled living room with its pine chairs, pine dining room table and pine cocktail table. There were pine place mats, pine bowls, and pine wood waiting to be burned in the fire place.

The walls were decorated with pine carvings of owls and seagulls. And when I used their bathroom, I could smell the pine scented shampoo and soaps. A small, green, plastic pine tree hung above the toilet to give a pine scent to anything accomplished there.

There was so much pine in their home that I wasn't sure if they loved the wood and the smell of balsam or hated the trees so much that they wanted to be almost single-handedly responsible for decimating them.

That afternoon, the three of us enjoyed what was commonly referred to as "Coffee and..." in the parlance of the area. The "And" could refer to as few as two cookies per person. Or, as was the case when Dottie was the hostess, "And' meant offering enough food to stock a truck stop for a month.

That morning she served cookies, rolls, butter, cheese, cheese balls, melted cheese on bread, chips, crackers, wedges of bologna, pickles and cucumber slices on bits of toast, a smattering of Chicken of the Sea, chicken wings, veggies and dip, lingonberries from their own bushes, local apples and strawberries, and a few knishes.

During my visit, Dottie got to talking about how she and Jim had met. He was a young teacher and she was his high school student. Dottie decided to "take him away" from his girlfriend, another teacher at the school.

When Jim went out to get more wine for our "Coffee and...", Dottie whispered that the secret of her success was dancing so close to him when he chaperoned the senior prom that he couldn't break away from her for fear of revealing "his enormous woody."

When she remembered her triumph, the sharpness of her expression made it clear that she still had the fierce competitiveness needed to win the heart of Jim Gerlund over half a century ago.

I had just eaten more of "And..." than someone concerned with developing hard muscle mass should, when Jim said, "How about a glass of Chateau Double Wide

Chablis? I keep the jugs downstairs where I have my collection of plants. I'd like to show them to you."

Jim and I went to the basement, leaving Dottie alone to put plastic wrap around the food. In the basement, we saw Jim's pride and joy -- a tall strange plant coming from a huge bulb dangling in mid-air above a container of swampy, rancid soil. The plant had a flower on top that looked like a black, suicidal calla lily or a diseased vagina that might guarantee virginity to any woman who had it.

According to Jim, this plant only bloomed "once every century."

With the self-satisfaction of an owner about to show off his dog's new trick, Jim insisted that I sample the aroma of this rare blossom.

I gamely leaned forward and tentatively inhaled. After one whiff, my head snapped back. Jim guffawed, "You got it. Smells like shit, don't it?"

I complimented Jim, "Your triumphs make me feel horticulturally challenged."

He replied humbly, "Anyone would."

I decided that, after this experience in male bonding, I could bring up forbidden topics. "Look, Jim," I said, "we're both manly men and we understand the ways of the males. I'll cut right to the chase: was Jerry Andrews jumping your wife's bones? And did his poaching piss you off?"

Jim surprised me with his candidness when he admitted, "Oh, hell, it was just once, it was maybe 12 or 15 years ago, and Jerry and I had a nice, friendly discussion about it."

I wanted to know all about that discussion.

Jim continued, "He said it was just something he had to do -- put the blocks to every woman who crossed his path. Jerry was very apologetic. He was Catholic, and he went on and on about how guilty he felt and all. So he went to the priest, Father Damian, to talk about the terrible burden of his unnaturally huge schlong."

I asked him what the priest advised Jerry to do.

Jim sadly remembered, "Jerry began to cry when he said that the priest wanted to examine the 'instrument of the devil.'"

According to Jim, Jerry opened the little window between the rooms of the confessional, unzipped his pants, and knelt on the bench so he could show his monster to the priest.

Well, that priest began praying and thanking the Holy Mother for the miracle and for the magnificent table that She had set for him. Then the priest began anointing Satan's torture instrument. As Jerry described it, first the guy sprinkled it with holy water, then Jerry was rubbed with holy oil, and finally Jerry was screaming, 'Holy cow!'"

The priest's cure only helped him for a couple of hours, but he never went back to the church with his problem again. Jim said, "I often wonder if Jerry would be a happier man today if he had gone back and allowed that priest's prayers to be answered again and again."

According to Jim, Jerry tried to be good until taken over by the force of his member, something that happened all the time. "I felt sorry for him because he complained about being unable to control himself. That is, I felt sorry for him until he asked if he could screw my wife again. Then I wanted to put him out of his misery.

"But Jerry was the Old Unfaithful of Sex, needing something almost every hour. It affected his wife, who became a horrible drunk. And his kids, all of whom were delinquents. And all because of the bulge in his pants."

I asked, "It seems like you'd almost be doing him a favor if you just cut it off for him."

"Thought about doing just that," Jim matter of factly shook his head. He said, "I'd do it only as a favor to Jerry. I

92

was actually studying up to see if I could transplant it to myself--not that I'd ever want Jerry's problems and I'd be too embarrassed to go to a doctor to do a thing like that. But I was quietly taking home study courses in self-transplantation. The kit that I got said that all I needed was an Exacto knife, rubbing alcohol and ordinary needle and thread. All I wanted to do, you see, was to understand Jerry by feeling what it would be like to be him for a couple of hours."

I tried to show him I understood. I said, "You wanted to walk a mile in his shoes."

Jim sadly shook his head and corrected, "It would be more accurate to say I wanted to hump with a smile in strange cooze. I never did any of it, never graduated from the study courses, never even transplanted a frog's leg to another frog. And I hated myself for letting that monster walk amongst us without ever knowing who he really was."

"Are you suggesting that the priest might want to harm Jerry because Jerry never returned with his instrument of the devil?" I squinted at Jim. I have learned that squints either make the detective seem threatening or terribly near-sighted.

Jim demurred, "Not exactly. All I'm saying is that most churches want to have religious artifacts, the jetsam and flotsam of the bodies of saints. A toenail here, a fingernail there, a wart in a gold case, a femur on display for centuries--the stuff of miracles. I believe that anyone, including Father Damian, who took the time to gaze on Jerry's magnificent member would believe in the existence of the devil. And would want to see it again and again to encourage them in the battle against evil."

The suspect list had enlarged to include Father Damian and any clergymen to whom Jerry might have shown his hammer. But Jim had unwittingly put himself deeper under suspicion with the admission that he didn't like Jerry playing the two-humped, priapic camel driver with his wife.

We climbed the steps from the basement to rejoin Dottie, who chided us, "Welcome back, boys. I'm assuming you had a wonderful time talking about women's private parts the way all men do. Tony, have you forgotten your appointment to stop the pissers in the woods?"

Before I could stammer a response, Uncle Guido and Pro were knocking at the door.

Uncle Guido greeted the Gerlunds with, "How's your lingonberries hanging?"

I grinned proudly. My Uncle Guido was always able to talk to anyone and everyone about the topics that interested them the most.

Then Uncle Guido turned to me, "We got some news for you, champ. How's about we have a little private conference?"

Dottie interrupted, "We were just talking about stopping the kids from whizzing in the woods and I have yet to get an assurance from Mr. Testa as to when he will address himself to that task."

The normally silent Pro whispered, "They will not be a problem after tonight."

Dottie stuttered, "But how?"

Uncle Guido added, "Consider the matter settled. I will personally help my nephew put an end to the degradations."

Dottie asked, "We do not have a lot of money. What do we owe you for this service?"

"Nothing, now," Uncle Guido said. "But in the future I may ask a small favor of you. That time may never come, but..."

"Marlon Brando," I shouted. "'The Godfather,' right?"

"A masterpiece," Uncle Guido said. "It changed my life."

Dottie insisted, "What would you ask of us?"

Uncle Guido assured, "Do not worry about that. A little nothing--a stack of lingonberry pancakes or a smile on a winter's day, a bit of tongue action at the front door, or a quick dry hump in the back of a Chevy. Nothing you would ever miss. But that day may never come, and come to think of it, I might never either."

Jim suddenly seemed worried. He said, "They're just kids, the wood pissers. I wouldn't want them hurt."

Uncle Guido guaranteed, "Not hurt, they just need to be housebroken."

As we left, I could see Dottie and Jim holding each other and looking quite concerned as if they were not sure about the force that they had unleashed. I almost went back to tell them that Uncle Guido or Pro never killed anyone that didn't need killing, but I realized that might only needlessly worry them even more.

As the three of us walked down the hill, I asked, "Not wanting to pry, but just how are you going to help me accomplish this task?"

Uncle Guido was confident, "There is an old adage that might be Chinese or whatever. It says: man cannot piss while someone throws firecrackers at his pecker. With a little more fire power, we'll teach them to keep their pants zipped in the woods for years to come."

I nodded in quick acceptance of another brilliant Uncle Guido plan.

Uncle Guido continued, "About that Popsicle in your basement. We've been asking around."

I nodded. Of course I knew what Uncle Guido was talking about. I have been around my uncle long enough to realize that a lot of his conversation has to be coded to avoid police wire taps and the like.

He continued, "We know the message but we aren't sure of the messenger."

Pro rasped, "When we are, we erase the messenger, right boss?"

Uncle Guido was quickly angry, "The boy doesn't have to know the details."

Pro looked chagrinned.

Uncle Guido continued, "I've been involved in a little side line, a little nothing to keep me occupied until something bigger comes along. We've been fixing the price of one-of-a-kind zircon wedding rings on eBay by bidding them up to artificial highs. Your dead man, Jerry whatshisname, wasn't pretending to be Geronimo with those freaky shoes. We think he was dressed like Cupid. The message is that someone didn't enjoy our little side business and wants cubic zirconium to return to its natural cheap price. For all we know, it was some guy who was upset about spending $34.95 on a diamond wedding ring."

I stopped in my tracks. I leaned close to Uncle Guido and said, "Out of complete respect for you and your opinions, I still have to ask why would anyone want to fix the price of zircon?"

Uncle Guido snapped back at me, "For the same reason men climb Mount Everest. Because it is there."

"But why would anyone kill another human being to warn you to stop doing that?"

"Who knows?" Uncle Guido said. "Maybe he can't spell and doesn't want to write threatening notes for fear people would make fun of him. Maybe he's shy. Who said people do the strangest things?"

I answered, "I think it was Art Linkletter, but I don't think he was talking about murderers who leave half naked bodies in someone else's living room. Can't you think of any other reasons why anyone would want to kill Jerry Andrews?"

Uncle Guido was silent for a moment as he pursed his lips thoughtfully. Then he said, "Look, that's what we heard

96

on the street today. It may not be the final answer and we still don't have the name of the jamoke who was pissed off enough to leave a message like that."

Pro rumbled, "When we do...."

"Right," agreed Uncle Guido. "Find the messenger, hit the erase button, end of the problem. Capeesh?"

We were walking through the winding roads of Sears Point. The oak, maple and elm trees made a green canopy over our heads. The wild flowers seemed sprayed on the hillsides. It was in this peaceful, restful place that my Uncle Guido was talking about "erasing" someone from this life and sending him into the next.

To get his mind off murder, I mentioned that a guy had leaped out from behind a tree to sucker punch me before I talked to Freedom Plenty. I described him as "Some crazed Watchtower salesman who told me not to be a buttinsky."

Uncle Guido and Pro treated that threat very seriously. Uncle Guido said, "Sounds like a message from Droopy Dick. It's the way he operates. Maybe we should call upon him."

"Droopy Dick?" I said. "I thought you gave out nicknames yourselves so no one would get that kind of a moniker."

"We do," Uncle Guido answered, sadly. "But some things can't be avoided. If you ever saw him in a shower, you'd know it was a perfect and unavoidable nickname. Even his four wives called him Droopy Dick. "

"Now don't get me wrong," I said. "I handled myself pretty well and the fist that he used to hit me upside the head will be sore for a long time. But I think I need a silent, vicious, dangerous sidekick like the other detectives have."

Without waiting for their response, I continued, "I've done some studying on this.

"Spencer has Hawk, his big black terribly efficient friend in most of the Robert B. Parker books. They crack jokes and then, when the going gets roughest, Hawk saves Spencer's ass.

"In the James Patterson novels, his hero Alex Cross has his big police buddy named John Sampson. Serial killers seem to be in every corner in their books and Sampson does his best to protect Alex Cross.

"In the Robert Crais books, his hero Elvis Cole has Joe Pike, described as 'the world's largest two-legged pit bull.'

"Hell, even female detectives, like Stephanie Plum, the girl bounty hunter, has sidekicks like Morelli (who she likes and doesn't like), Ranger (the strong, silent type) and even her grandmother.

"It seems to me I'm missing out on a trend and some day it could save my life. My dog, Mr. Jake the Clever Canine, would rather stay home and watch the Animal Channel on cable. And I'd settle for any kind of a sidekick, even a chicken, if it could be attack trained."

I was out of breath when I finished explaining my needs. Then the silence was deafening except for my Uncle Guido, who sadly shook his head and whispered, "He wants an attack-trained chicken."

I looked at Uncle Guido and Pro, and thought I detected a little sadness coming from them. For all I knew, they might have been pooped, hung over, depressed, suffering from indigestion, too much Merry Martha or something like that, but they sure looked dejected to me.

Trying to get some psychological insight into their often hidden emotions while attempting to lighten the mood, I asked, "What happened? Did someone step on your yet-to-be dug grave?"

After another long pause, Pro took me aside, walking about ten feet into a hill filled with Dutchmen's Britches. (By the way, from looking at those flowers I conclude that the Dutch, who wore underwear like that, had to be very studly or every time they took off their pantaloons the girls would laugh at them.)

He nodded in the direction of Uncle Guido, who was looking away from us, and whispered, "You hurt his feelings. And mine."

"Who me? All I said was..."

"Shhh," he shushed. "I know what the fuck you said. What you don't know is what's going on in your Uncle Guido's life these days."

"So tell me," I said. "You got my attention."

Pro sighed, "This is very tough to say and I wish I didn't have to tell it to you. You think of your Uncle Guido as The Godfather, but his life is more like the Sopranos. One of his sons, Secundo, turned out to be gay. That's not so bad, but Secundo is living with the gay son of Guido's biggest enemy, a leader of the Scrotari gang. How do you think he feels about that?

"His wife wants him to retire to Sun City, but he wants to stay in the business. So she's got two of them going to a marriage counselor. Also, because this shrink has a big mouth, now everyone in the organization knows that the man needs seven Viagra pills a day just to keep his pecker up. Seven. Do you know what a thing like that does to a made man's reputation?"

I offered, "It didn't hurt Bob Dole, a former presidential candidate, when he did those Viagra commercials."

"All right," Pro said. "But look at Dole's wife. Everyone gives him credit for even trying to stand up in the face of that."

I had to agree.

"Your Uncle Guido is a giant in his business," Pro continued. "Did you know that he was the only three-time winner of the Intimidator of the Year Trophy in the history of the annual Gangster Awards?"

"I never knew that," I admitted. "Wow! The Gangster Awards!"

"We'll take you next time," Pro said. "Held every year since 1902 at a new undisclosed location. Winners get Momos, statues named for Giancana. 'Tonys,' as an honor to Accardo, would have been a better name than the Momo, but Tonys already go to sissy boys in Broadway shows. Your uncle would have gotten the Coveted Lucky Luciano Life Plus 100 Years Achievement Award but for some Scrotari plotting."

"Those damn Scrotaris," I said, without thinking.

"Shhh," Pro protested. "Your Uncle Guido has feelings, too. Now don't let him know that I talked to you about this, but go over, apologize and ask him to be your sidekick."

"He's standing only five feet away," I pointed out. "He's got to see that you're whispering and spitting in my ear."

"Sorry about that," Pro said, "I'm one of those wet whisperers. Just do it, OK?"

So I turned to Uncle Guido and said, "A little birdy tells me you're upset that I might want someone else to be my big, vicious sidekick."

For some reason Pro was shaking his head back and forth as if he had water in his ears.

I continued, "Look, I can handle myself in most situations, but would you like to be my sidekick if something serious comes up?"

I never saw my Uncle Guido with a grin quite that wide. There might have been a tear in his eye as he said, "I'd be proud to." He hugged me so hard that it nearly squeezed the breathe out of me.

Then I remembered, "This would be like those books where the female bounty hunter named Stephanie Plum is helped by her grandmother, who enjoys going to funeral homes to see how well the body is laid out."

"Only difference with me on board," my Uncle Guido clarified, "is that, while I wouldn't mind visiting funeral homes with you, chances are we'd be the ones providing the body."

100

After we all had a little laugh, Pro said, "And I can be the assistant side kick, OK?"

When I agreed, Pro joined in the hugging. The three of us were crying, smiling and kissing each other on the ears and foreheads when Merry Martha walked past us. She said, "I thought it was something like that."

And it was a little upsetting to hear her mutter as she left us, "A woman can only count on her dog these days."

Chapter Five

Which was the reason Uncle Guido and I stayed up all night hugging our shotguns and waiting for some kid to piss in the woods.

When I told my Uncle Guido about all the cases that needed my attention, he agreed that I should try to focus my energies on the most important ones. His memorable advice was, "Getting rid of the little shit gives you time for the big shits."

We figured that kids pissing in the woods was the easiest job to quickly complete. So that night we waited for an overflowing bladder to lure a partygoer out of the Clement house.

We were watching from under the low branches of a huge pine tree. The mosquitoes were gleefully accepting our blood donations and there wasn't much to do but fitfully slap at them, keep an eye on the house, and try to stay awake.

This gave me a chance to really talk to my Uncle Guido and I was grateful for that. As we waited, our conversation meandered through many topics: sex, women, breasts, legs, lubricity and business strategy.

As we spoke, I remembered quotations from books I'd been assigned to read in college. Our time together gave me a chance to check out my Uncle Guido's reactions to the accepted wisdom taught in business schools.

For instance, I told Uncle Guido about the book in which the respected writer commented: "Don't assume the harvest is in hand just because the seeds are in the ground..."

Uncle Guido's response was brief, "This mutt don't know shit. What the fuck is he talking about? Hire a fuckin' gardener. I'm askin' some guy where's the fuckin' vig he owes me, and he comes out wit' 'don't assume the harvest is at hand just because the seeds are in the ground', he gets zotzed. He's in the ground with his fucking seeds. End of story."

Then I mentioned an important book on leadership that made its author a rich, respected man and an acclaimed speaker. That book advised: "The basic principles of effective leadership are: give a man a fish and you feed him for a day. Teach him to fish and you feed him for a lifetime."

Uncle Guido enthusiastically responded, "Now we're gettin' somewhere. Then you tell him 25 fuckin' percent of the fish he catches he brings to you, or he sleeps with the other 75 percent."

That night my Uncle Guido said, "You wanna know the personal saying that has given me the greatest I strength? Now you remember this for all time. It is: I put you in the ground before you put me in the ground."

What a great uncle-nephew conversation! So full of warmth and sharing.

I also told him that I remembered some good advice advocated in a very popular business book. That book told its readers, "Don't fish for trout in a goldmine or pan for gold in a trout stream."

Uncle Guido chided me, "See this is the problem with America. You got jerkoffs like this sayin' 'don't fish for trout in a goldmine' and dumb fucks goin' around thinkin' that's some relevant shit. Look, the only guy I know who would get behind that crap is maybe Wally the Nose, but he's got a plate in his head."

What, then, did Uncle Guido offer to replace the storehouse of contemporary business wisdom? Among his most noteworthy precepts that he shared with me that night were:

* don't piss where you eat.

* don't make fart sounds with your arm pits during normal business hours.

• everyone wipes his own ass.

Uncle Guido also had enlightened ideas about worker benefits: "In my outfit, we ain't got no medical coverage, psychiatric care, dental, or gynecological benefits unless I perform them myself. And yet people are constantly asking to enter my association.

"Our primary benefits are what make sense to people: we can park where the fuck we want, broads are attracted to us, and we have early, permanent, silent retirement if you fuck up."

In many ways, Uncle Guido exemplified modern-day managerial benevolence and generosity. For instance, that night he told me, "You can use my Chicago Bulls basketball tickets on any night that I'm busy. Now that they got rid of Jordan, you can go every night because I don't fuckin' care about them."

Once again I was in awe of my Uncle Guido's simple wisdom. I was, in fact, in thrall with him even though I'm not sure what it means. If it has anything to do with anything sexual, then it's the wrong word. But if it means, as I suspect it does, that I love, respect and honor my Uncle Guido, then I am indeed "In thrall." I am, in fact, fully thralled.

My Uncle Guido even left me with one last memorable bit of wisdom, "Always be the last one to check your weapons at the door."

I knew I could spend the rest of my life pondering the implications of that one sentence and not explore all the possible ways it could make me a more effective person.

I was about to reveal to him that, if my detection work in Sears Point was successful, I'd like to begin franchising the idea everywhere in the country. I wanted to listen to his suggestions about setting up a new business.

Before I could open that subject, my Uncle Guido punched me in the shoulder. Hard. Before I could whimper, "Ouch," I saw that he was pointing just beyond the Clement house.

At first I didn't see what he had noticed. I stared at the driveway that ran alongside the house and saw nothing out of the ordinary. When I turned to ask Uncle Guido what was up, he put his left hand over my mouth and continued to point.

Then I saw it. Skulking along beside the Clement house, sneaking an approach to the Clement garbage cans was a masked marauder, a garbage-strewing raccoon.

I held my breath and slowly raised my already cocked shotgun. Uncle Guido did the same until we had considerable firepower aimed at the critter that George Svoboda wanted us to stop.

We both held our breaths.

We both began to apply pressure on the triggers.

We were about to send that raccoon into the well-lit tunnel that leads to his heaven's easy-to-tip garbage cans.

That was when a skinny guy with his cigarettes rolled into the sleeve of his T-shirt and his baggy pants barely hanging on to his butt staggered out of the Clement house and loped down the stairs. He seemed to need to get somewhere fast.

The raccoon sat up on its haunches on alert.

The skinny guy had his fly undone before his feet reached the bottom of the three stairs leading up to the Clement house.

The raccoon became more tense.

The skinny guy cut across the Clement front yard and was heading diagonally towards a big bush beside the driveway. His path would take him away from the street light that was in front of the third house to my right. It would also eventually take him away from the raccoon. But not soon enough.

The raccoon's eyes never left the skinny guy.

The skinny guy was cutting directly in front of the raccoon, blocking the critter from our vantage point.

I looked over to Uncle Guido, who was leaning forward, his finger on the trigger.

I was going to ask what we should do, but I decided I had better keep my eye on the scene in front of us. I also figured that as long as I did what Uncle Guido did, I'd be all right. So I, too, leaned forward.

When the skinny skeddadler was only a few feet from the bush, I could see the beginning of a yellow stream coming from the guy's crotch. Seeing that certainly ruined the ambiance of the evening.

Uncle Guido's shotgun fired. Blam! The silence of the night was ripped by the explosive sound.

My finger tightened involuntarily on the trigger. Without thinking about it, my shotgun also fired and the blast was nearly at the same time as Uncle Guido's.

Because my shotgun wasn't seated properly in my shoulder, the recoil knocked me backwards. For a fraction of a second I could not see the scene in front of me.

When I re-opened my eyes, I could see the raccoon scampering off to the left. It was heading to the safety of a group of trees.

The skinny guy was also running, only he was heading to the right. He was trying to get back to the house as fast as his legs could carry him.

106

The yellow stream had completely stopped, dammed up by twin shotgun blasts and whatever pellets peppered the skinny guy and his skinnier member.

Uncle Guido racked another shell. So did I.

Uncle Guido fired at the fleeing raccoon, sending up a huge spray of gravel and sand where the animal had been a fraction of a second before.

I also pulled the trigger, but it was more in reaction to the sound of Uncle Guido's blast than anything else. If I hit anything, it would only be a bird in the wrong place at the wrong time.

The skinny guy leaped up the three steps in a single bound, his pecker flapping in the breeze, and disappeared inside the Clement house. There were screams from the house. I guess it was bad etiquette to enter a late-night party with your fly completely unzipped.

I smelled a rather distinct odor and quickly understood what it was. The noise of our shotguns had so frightened the raccoon that we had scared the shit out of it. Literally.

Then I noticed a long, dark, tube-like object steaming on the steps leading into the Clement house. We'd had the same effect on the skinny guy.

Uncle Guido racked another shell. So did I.

But the skinny guy was gone. So was the raccoon.

Uncle Guido fired anyway. So did I and this time the butt of the shotgun did not bruise my shoulder.

To this day I'm not sure which of our shells did the damage, but both garbage cans outside the Clement house suddenly leaped into the air and tumbled over. And over.

Garbage was strewn over a 30 square yard area as bags burst, tin cans went flying and banana peels flopped through the air. The place looked like it had been decimated by the biggest, meanest raccoon of all time.

Lights were going on in homes throughout Sears Point. There was the sound of scampering feet as naked men, who were enjoying the comfort of a spouse other than their own, ran terrified back to their own homes. Wrong-bedded women returned to the warmth of their hubbies. In short, infidelity effectively and temporarily ended that night in Sears Point. I suppose a sustained shotgun volley at 2:15 A. M. would have a similar effect anywhere in the world.

Uncle Guido stood and surveyed the area in front of us. He said, "That raccoon will think twice before trying to get into a garbage can in these parts."

I proudly stood next to him. I spoke in a laconic fashion as if this were the end of a western starring John Wayne or Gary Cooper, "And that there skinny guy ain't going to urinate in the woods tonight--or maybe ever."

Uncle Guido clapped me on the shoulder and said, "Two problems solved. A good night's work. It's Miller time."

"That," I said smiling, "Or we're going to Disneyland."

We were smiling as we walked, two males bonded because of jobs well done.

On the way to my parents' home, several pajama-clad neighbors asked if we'd heard gun shots. Although we were carrying the shotguns, we told anyone who asked, "Didn't hear a thing."

Chapter Six

We were striding back home, triumphant, with a shared sense of accomplishment for jobs well done. We stopped in front of the door to my parent's weekend home while I got out my keys.

That was when I heard a low, mysterious sound. Ever alert, ever ready for trouble, ever able to sniff out danger when it lurks nearby, I asked Uncle Guido, "Did you fart?"

"Who me?" He asked incredulously. "I don't think so."

"Can you prove it?" I thought I had him there, but he came back with one of his amazing Uncle Guido retorts.

"OK, wise guy. Let's have a smell check," he said. "Right here, right now. It is well known that farts smell far worse to someone else than to yourself. Go ahead, Mr. Sensitive Nose, you go first and tell me what you smell."

Since that seemed fair enough, I turned my head to inhale in the general direction where that ozone destroyer might have originated if I were the culprit. I was confident of victory and absolutely sure I would only detect the aroma of the night air.

Uncle Guido did the same thing at precisely the same time. I can honestly say that, if I had not accused my Uncle Guido of whiffing a secret woofer, at that moment we both would be dead and this story would never be told.

In rapid succession, two arrows came out of the night, buzzing inches from our ears. We both heard the solid clunks as their points embedded themselves into the door.

We leaped to opposite sides of the doorway. I fell into a rose bush, where in rough emulation of the Lord who got a crown of thorns, I got an ass full of them!

When I voiced my pain and torment with the smallest of groans and whispered the quasi-religious invocation of "Keee-rist," another arrow came out of the darkness and broke the living room window just above my head.

I heard Uncle Guido, who had jumped into a skinny lilac bush on the other side of the doorway, rack a shell into his shotgun.

I quickly unhooked myself from the rose bush, hit the ground and cocked my shotgun.

Uncle Guido fired and almost immediately I could hear our next door neighbor, old Mr. Olson, who claimed he hadn't had a good night's sleep since seeing "Night of the Living Dead" in 1974, complaining, "Damn it, you kids stop blowing off them fireworks at this time of night."

I whispered, "Where is he?"

"Don't know," Uncle Guido whispered back, "But if you can't kill him, scare him to death." More great advice that I wanted to write down, but there was no time for that. I fired my shotgun in the general direction of somewhere in front of us.

Mr. Olson yelled, "Assholes," and we heard something big crashing through the bushes to our left. It was moving away from us.

We each fired and the music of that night went like this:

Blam!! "Assholes."

Blam!!! "Fucking assholes."

Silence.

110

"Shit heads."

It could have been the start of a symphony of violence and anger (I like that phrase, even though it has little to do with what was going on at the time), but that was the end of the attack.

Whoever was firing arrows at us crashed away into the darkness until the sounds from that direction diminished to only the faintest pitta-pat of a terrorist's footfalls.

And my first thought was, "It's about time."

I could have predicted that he would be out there somewhere. Watching, because he would be the kind of person who enjoyed watching. (Actually, he was a little late. My survey of recent novels indicated that on average the serial killer was introduced by page nine. And often Mr. Serial Killer was featured on page one.)

Waiting because waiting was what he did so well. He was also good at stalking. Slobbering. Drooling. Hanging around. Hocking. Hacking. Hulking.

How did I know? Because shit happens and this was the moment for the serial killer to make his (or rarely her) appearance in these cases. This vicious, amoral, disgusting human Dumpster would probably threaten someone I love or myself. This would traditionally give me the reason to get really angry and badly hurt the evil guy in the last page of any contemporary book that intends to be a thriller.

At least, that is the way it has worked in every best-selling exploration of the criminal mind for the last decade or more. So many authors and screen writers have made so much money off of crazed serial killers that I'm surprised that the murderers don't demand a piece of the action.

I crept out of that rose bush as soon as I was sure the bow-and-arrow hunter was gone. My key was in my trembling hand. I unlocked the door from a deep crouch so as to keep my head down just in case there was another arrow out there with my name on it.

But the image of that serial killer infected my mind and took over my thoughts. As he skulked away, about now his or her thinking would go something like this: "Hello, Tony, I'm your serial killer. I want to render you, skin you alive and eat you with candied yams. Or maybe boiled with last week's white socks and a touch of cumin for seasoning.

"Because I'm so diabolical, I can afford to arouse myself. I sing little ditties as I murder people. Songs like 'When a Killer Meets a Victim, A'Comin' Through the Rye.' Or 'I've Got Your Skin Over My Skin'... I'll have to work on that one, but you get the idea.

"I can read your mind. Be still now. Delving deeply, deeply. My, my, my, you still do that? Some day you'll grow hair on the palms of your hands if you keep that up!

"What do I want from you? Not much. A little terror. Some night sweats. Maybe, if you felt like it, you could piss in your pants at the thought of me. Ha, ha, ha, that was just a little joke.

"What I actually want is a huge movie and publishing contract with a fat advance. Work on that, Tony Baloney, and I'll let you live a little longer. Perhaps for a day or two. Until one of Cupid's arrows dispatches you to hell where you belong. Ha, ha, ha."

With thoughts like that, I was lucky to be able to get the key anywhere near the lock. Fortunately, that entire imaginary serial killer monologue flashed through my nimble mind in a fraction of a second. Frighten me and you put my mind into overdrive.

I know, I know. Instead of imagining the inner life of a serial killer, at that moment I should have been caring about my uncle, deepening my relationship with him, worrying about his safety, and maybe even hitting him up for a few bucks to tide me over until the really big money came in from franchising my small-town detecting agency concept.

I did remember to open the door for Uncle Guido and let him enter the safety of the house before me. That should count for something and it did -- for about a nanosecond. Uncle Guido thanked me for the courtesy and preceded me into the house in a crouched position so as to make a smaller target of himself.

That was when he tripped over another almost naked, obviously dead man.

As he was falling, Uncle Guido spun around and somehow landed face down on the body's back.

It is an absolute rule of life that you never, ever have a camera handy when you really need one. The thought occurred to me that, If I only had a picture of my Uncle Guido sprawled out on the back of a naked man, I would never have to work again. To keep that picture away from his friends and associates, Uncle Guido would surely pay me enough to make me a man of leisure.

So it was with some disappointment that I turned my attention to the new corpse in my parent's living room. He was wearing only construction boots. This stiff's hands were resting lightly on top of his head as if he were trying to confirm that he had just lost his hat to the wind they call Mariah.

Uncle Guido shouted, "What the fuck?" So typical of Uncle Guido.

I yelled, "Careful. Don't lose yourself in his ass."

"No fuckin' way. Is that what you did with the other one?" Uncle Guido asked. "That's disgusting. Be glad no one saw you, because people will talk."

"Why me?" I inquired. "Why this house? Why is this body here? Why now? Why is there death? Why do birds suddenly appear? Why?"

Uncle Guido got up, quickly walked over to me, slapped me, and said, "Get ahold of yourself."

I got very quiet after I said the obligatory, "Thanks, I needed that."

I thought we were just about to ratchet up the uncle-nephew bonding, when Pro showed up. He looked at the corpse and immediately observed, "Uglier shoes."

This was something that could not be denied. Although some people think construction boots are stylish, these were particularly large and clunky in a tan color resembling what you didn't want to look at in the toilet.

As a detective, I noticed that Pro had walked into the house with no apparent difficulties. I said, "Pro, my man, you don't need us to remove any arrows from your person, do you?"

"No," he said, "Should I?"

"Well someone was taking target practice on my uncle and me just a few minutes ago and..."

Pro immediately drew his huge .45 pistol and began backing around the living room. "You OK, boss?" he asked, expressing real concern while ignoring the fact that I'd had as many arrows shot at me as Uncle Guido had.

After Uncle Guido assured his human guard dog that he was fine, he waved in the general direction of the body and asked, "Why strangle someone after forcing them to wear bad shoes?"

"Good question," I said. It was, to be perfectly honest, the least I could say under the circumstances. "Of course, he could have been wearing the shoes before he was killed."

Uncle Guido asked, "Would that make any difference?"

"It would have made it much more difficult to get his clothes off," I surmised. Pro gave me an appreciative grin indicating that he was impressed with my deductive reasoning.

Since I knew a little about these things, I added, "Also, if either corpse was wearing their shoes before they were killed, they would have great difficulty accessorizing."

114

"Yah, I'd hate to have to think of what to wear with moccasins or those construction brogans," Pro observed. Then he theorized, "Could be that there's a crazed totally fucked up killer who also needs to get rid of inventory from a bad shoe store."

I shook my head, "Excuse me, but that seems a little far fetched. Have you ever known of anyone who would kill people so he could fit them with bad shoes?"

Uncle Guido offered, "No, but I do say that there's a first for everything."

Another great phrase, another time when I did not have a pencil or a piece of paper.

Uncle Guido said, "Answer the ugly shoe question and you might solve two murders -- and keep your Uncle Guido alive."

"You?" I beseeched. "You still think this is some kind of a message for you?"

Uncle Guido gave me a withering look that suggested that I had wasted the price of a college education and still only had the IQ of cactus.

"If it ain't no message," Pro opined, "It's a shame. It's just a waste of a couple of perfectly good bodies."

"Uncle Guido, did you ever wear ugly shoes?" I knew I was grasping at straws, but I had to explore every avenue. "If this is a 'message,' maybe someone is telling you something about your taste in footwear?"

"Leave my fuckin' footwear out of this, or I'll put my size 12 Florsheims right up your ass."

Uncle Guido was exasperated, even though he probably didn't know the meaning of the word. He glared at me and said, "We got another dead motherfucker in the living room and we got to do something about it. Soon."

He paused, gave me a stare that would wilt lettuce two miles away in a well-watered field and pointedly added,

"Without anyone accusing their relatives or partners of bad taste. Kapeesh? Any suggestions from my brain trust?"

My Testosteroni testosterone was getting pretty active about then. I mean, Uncle Guido was my sidekick. I was supposed to be in charge and he was supposed to be my brain-and-muscle trust. And now he was giving orders to me and being sarcastic about it.

I felt like giving him a piece of my mind and firing him as my sidekick, but then I thought better of it. My dad once told me that once you have a deal with The Organization, that's it. For life. They might end the association with you, but it never, ever goes the other way.

Let me explain: The Organization resembles getting on the mailing lists for catalogues for clothing outlets or signing up with AOL. Once you're part of their system, it is almost impossible to unsnarl yourself from them.

Since I could not fire Uncle Guido from my organization without serious consequences from his, I figured the way to get Uncle Guido's mind back on track was to involve him in the detecting process.

I said, "I've got two quick ideas. First, maybe the arrows have a clue as to who is firing them at us. Maybe someone should look at them?"

When I said that I was remembering those old time cowboy movies. When John Wayne looked at any arrow, he'd immediately know what tribe made it, who fired it, was the warrior who fired it right or left handed and did he love his squaw.

"In second place," I continued, "I still have that Sheriff Clem problem, so it is doubly necessary to hide the second body until we know the identity of the killer and why he or she uses my parent's home as a morgue."

"That's my nephew," Uncle Guido said proudly. "Taught him everything he knows and now he's teaching me a few things. Pro, you're head of our body disposal section. Tony and me'll check out those arrows."

116

As Pro went through his checklist--any highways being built (no), any big holes being dug (no), any bottomless swamps around (no), Uncle Guido and I tiptoed to the front door.

I quickly opened it, grabbed the three arrows embedded in it, ducked, jumped back into the house and slammed the door shut.

We put the arrows on the dining room table. Sure enough, the first arrow had a small piece of paper rolled around the shaft and held in place by a small rubber band. I removed the rubber band and opened the paper, read it to myself and, like a jury foreman passing the verdict on to the judge, gave it to Uncle Guido.

The paper said, "Not this one, dummy, look at other arrow."

My always colorful Uncle Guido muttered, "This mope deserves to die on a rotisserie with a hot poker up his ass."

Uncle Guido immediately grabbed for the next arrow. It, too, had a rubber band around another piece of paper. Uncle Guido opened it, instantly said the word, "Shit," and passed the paper to me. This time the arrow's message was, "Not this one, you dumb fuck, the other one."

Now even I was getting angry. Uncle Guido hit the table so hard the cow creamer gurgled without having any milk in it.

I grabbed the third arrow before Uncle Guido could reduce it to toothpicks. Another note was held to the shaft with another rubber band.

The third note said:

"(To be spoken with a white boy's rap beat)

This note is a clue

Here's what you do

Bang your head against a wall

Until on the floor you fall

And hold your breath and turn bright blue.

Screw you, screw you, screw you.

You are so dumb I can't believe it.

Your brains are zeros and you're a shit."

Now I joined Uncle Guido in his anger. How dare this two-bit, cow humping, teat sucking, fly sniffing, clod humping (did I use the word "humping" already --sorry, because when swearing it is a point of honor not to use the same word twice), clod pumping, shoe licking son of a bitch try to make the world's future greatest detective feel bad?

But then, almost as soon as my anger kicked in, my deductive reasoning took charge. I examined the "Poem" and, besides finding it wanting when compared to any of the Dr. Seuss oeuvre, I noticed a pattern here and an indication of personality there.

"What ho," I said, reflecting my notion that anything said with a British accent is more acceptable than anything said from the heart of America, "Yoiks, look here. The meter of the poem doesn't scan and the word usage is suspect. We could make some assumptions here, I dare say we could."

Uncle Guido said, "Stop talking like a fag and tell me what you see?"

"Just by looking at his poetic excesses," I announced, "I can tell that this guy is 5' 5" to 6' 1", blonde, was picked on in school, was cruel to animals before the eighth grade, read Playboy but not for the stories, drove a 1975 El Dorado for 15 minutes in 1986, suffers when teased on a date, loves burritos, has never read the Sunday New York Times from cover to cover, and is neither a member of a political party or a religious organization, although he reads the Bible."

"And how do you know all that?" asked Pro.

118

I was happy to inform him that I make those conclusions with my powers of deduction.

"For instance," I said, "from the way your shoulders are bent right now I can see that you are constipated and are thinking of taking a bowel movement. In fact, you can excuse yourself to go to the washroom right now, if you like. Am I right?"

Pro smiled wickedly and said, "No, no need of that. In fact I took a crap in the bushes by your front door just before I came in. What do you have to say to that?"

In no uncertain terms, I suggested, "Please use the back door from now on."

It was Uncle Guido who got us back on track and focused our attention on the dead body. He interrupted the demonstration of my deductive powers by asking Pro what his conclusions were about body disposal. Pro said, "All I could come up with on such short notice was another freezer somewhere."

"Wait," I offered. "Mrs. Clements has a freezer and a generator for providing electricity. Her kid is probably long gone now that Uncle Guido and I nearly shot off his whizzer. All we'd have to do to keep it running is to make sure the tank has enough diesel fuel."

Once my idea was accepted, we worked like a well-practiced team, which of course we were because this was the second body we were storing. I got the big, black plastic bags; Uncle Guido went over to the Clements house to get the generator started; Pro arranged the body so it would fit in the freezer.

After Uncle Guido got back and just before we were going to duct tape the bags shut, he asked, "So who the hell is this guy anyway?"

"Looks a little like Bottle Nose Scharpelli," Pro said.

"Couldn't be," Uncle Guido said. "Bottle Nose died tragically while he was masturbating into a fan belt just before that Banc 31 job. The amazing thing was that the widow allowed the fan belt mechanic to speak at the funeral."

I looked closely at the body for the first time since Uncle Guido had almost tripped over it. It looked a lot like Thurmond Howarth, who was one of those guys who'd had a great body in high school. If it was Thurmond, he had been going downhill ever since.

Thurmond was the person I most admired back then. Quarterback, forward on the basketball team, the guy who screwed all the cheerleaders in every sport, the coolest person who ever entered Millard Fillmore High.

(We always called ourselves M. F. High, although the teachers frowned on that abbreviation.)

It was even rumored that he'd copped the virginity of Prudence Farelly, who publicly vowed not to give up her most precious jewel until she had six gold records. After listening to her voice, most boys thought scaling that particular peak was a hopeless task and gave up. Not Thurmond, although to this day no one knows what he promised Prudence in exchange for her virginity. All we knew at the time was that it had to be more than Thurmond's collection of baseball trading cards.

His body now looked like he had not been keeping up his own temple in recent decades. His love handles drooped to his hips, his stomach proclaimed that this is where 10,000 beers resided. He was balding, with a blotchy rummy complexion. His teeth were yellow and he needed a shave -- a far cry from the lover boy who was the alpha male of my high school class.

Pro asked, "His name's Howarth?"

"That's him, I'm sure now," I opined, "And I'm sure of one other thing." (Dramatic pause inserted here, especially in the movie version of this book) "We're dealing with a serial killer."

120

(In your mind, please insert musical stinger here, with a battalion of basses being bowed so they sounded very ominous. In fact, I thought the moment required musical underlining. That was why I began to hum a single low tone, holding it for as long as I had a breath. Uncle Guido looked at me as if my head had suddenly developed a crack the size of the one in the liberty bell.)

"If I know anything about serial killers--and I know a lot just from reading James Patterson--they all have souvenir rooms where they keep press clippings, human parts and/or their victims' underwear," I said.

"Find the souvenir room and we probably won't instantly find the killer, but we'll have so many clues that we should be able to get him just before he disembowels someone we love. Happens all the time."

I guess I was persuasive because, as soon as we dumped Howarth's body in the Clements' freezer, we began a house-to-house search of the immediate vicinity. It wasn't easy knocking on doors and asking anyone who answered if they had any rooms dedicated to souvenirs of death and/or dismemberment. We got a lot of odd looks and not a few doors slammed in our faces.

One resident, Terry Kraus, who I had always thought was a little light in the heels, admitted to having a room dedicated to Judy Garland and to his Barbie Doll collection. He was immediately struck off any list of suspects. I figured that anyone who sang "Somewhere Over the Rainbow" couldn't be a serial killer, although several serial killers have been known to harbor a grudge against Ken.

Before Uncle Guido or Pro could protest my decision, I remembered another vital element. The serial killer's souvenir room had to be isolated, dusty, mysterious, frightening, never visited by a broom or mop and filled with spiders, mice, rats and, if possible, monstrous snakes.

The moment the detective walked into any room that was the lair of the serial killer, he knew two things: (1) this guy was a dangerous crazy and (2) no one could live there. It had to be a place where goofy people who like bugs, rodents and snakes hang out every now and then.

There was only one place anywhere in Saw Mill adjacency fitting that description. That was why we immediately went to the Abandoned Outhouse in the Woods (AOW).

When I was growing up and my parents were taking me to Sears Point during the summer, the AOW was the most frightening spot on earth, scarier by far than any haunted house in any carnival, more intimidating than coming home with a report card that required a parent to personally meet a teacher, and more frightening than looking at the mummies at the Field Museum and realizing that the plugs in their noses were put there after their brains were taken out through their nostrils (a sure way to stop any young boy from picking his nose).

It was a long, tall, narrow shack deep in the woods and it had a hole in the floor that we were told went straight to hell. Anyone falling in there never, ever came back.

If anyone walked close enough to the Abandoned Outhouse in the Woods, the smell was enough to induce dizziness. The odor alone was rumored to have killed an unwary telephone worker who had stumbled into the AOW while fending off a case of nervous colon.

The other boys told me (it was not something I ever cared to experience), if you dared get close enough to the AOW to put your ear to the wooden walls, you could hear strange sounds coming from within. Gurgling. Bubbling. And sometimes a low, throaty giggle of the devil himself.

Not that I ever believed any of that, but I pass it on to the reader so you can understand how concerned we were as we attempted to find the Abandoned Outhouse in the Woods.

While we searched, I remembered that I owed a progress report to Amanda. I almost suggested that I take care of business and let Uncle Guido and Pro proceed to the outhouse without me, but something stopped me.

Perhaps it was duty. Or the sense that I might be teased. A feeling that it would be worse to be called a coward by an esteemed member of my own family than to be kidnapped and held in the AOW.

It wasn't very difficult to find the outhouse. There were, in fact, signs saying "This way to Abandoned Outhouse in the Woods (AOW)."

I remarked about how easy kids had it these days with signs pointing the way. I said, "When I was a kid, we had nothing but our own nerve to help us find the outhouse."

Pro spat, "You had it easy. Shit, no one put an outhouse in the woods for us. In my day we had to build the shitters ourselves."

Uncle Guido bested both of us with, "You both had lives of leisure and ease. In my day, who knew from outhouses or from building them? From the day I was born, I was told to hold it until scientists could invent something to take care of that business. So I did. I held it until I was a teen ager. And let me tell you, 14 years of constipation is not easy."

Conversation like that made short work of our trek into the woods. In a few minutes, after walking up a small, tree-covered dune, we looked down into a valley and there it was: the creepy crapper.

I was personally amazed that there was no odor as we approached. Something must have purified the area. Perhaps it was a Good Samaritan, who had cleaned the outhouse and then died knowing that he had made this part of the world a safer place for anyone who really needed to take a dump. Perhaps it was just time that allowed the assembled roughage to return to its nitrogen roots and dissipate.

In any case, having gone to the epi-center of evil odors and smelled nothing that would cause me to faint, I decided that I would be the one to enter the Shitter of Death. Alone.

Uncle Guido tried to dissuade me, claiming that he could never face my father if I died in there. I bravely held his shoulder and announced, "If that happens, just tell the truth at the funeral. Tell them I died with my pants up."

I opened the door and quickly entered before Uncle Guido or Pro could stop me. It was dark and dank, but far from unpleasant.

The walls and even the ceiling were covered with graffiti including such classics as "You have the future of America in your hands," "Came to shit, thought I started, how sad, only farted," and "If you're reading this, you're probably pissing on your shoe."

Then I saw that one wall had been cleaned of graffiti. Someone had painted it white. On this wall, I could see a picture of an eye. To its right there was a caricature of what appeared to be Dan Rather, the CBS anchorman, followed by cartoons of a bee and a downhill skier.

Uncle Guido began pounding on the door. "Are you all right?" he shouted. "What did you do--stop to take a leek?"

"I'm fine," I answered. "Come in here quick and look at this."

They rushed in and stopped in their tracks when they saw the pictures on the wall. Pro best expressed what was on all our minds when he said, "What the fuck?"

But I was beginning to see a pattern. I said, "What if the eye isn't really an 'eye,' as in 'all-seeing eye'? What if the eye stood for the letter 'I'?"

Uncle Guido proudly said, "The kid's a genius. I woulda guessed that the 'eye' was supposed to be the beginning of 'eye-talian' or something like that. So what do you make of that anchorman? Maybe it stands for asshole, as in 'I, Asshole.' Wasn't there some television show called 'I, Claudius'? Could be that the asshole picked up that way of referring to himself."

I figured, "No, that would be too complicated. That's probably supposed to be a picture of Dan Rather. So the message so far is either 'I Dan' or 'I Rather.' Now the 'I Dan' could be pronounced 'Eden,' but why would someone put a reference to Eden on the wall of The Abandoned Outhouse in the Woods?"

Uncle Guido said, "Must be some crazy dumb fuck."

Pro and I were silently amazed. My uncle had cut through the candy bar of confusion to find the nougat of logic at the center.

Pro jumped in, "The next picture is of a bee, so maybe it's something about honey. Eden honey? Eating honey, which might be the name of a girl plus what the artist wants to do to her."

I pondered that. "Could be," I agreed. "It sounds like the kind of message someone would write on a bathroom wall, but if you did want to leave that message, why do it in pictures and why in some kind of code? It could be 'I', 'Dan', 'bee'. Like he's leaving us a name."

"'I'm Dan B' or indicating a one word name like 'I'm Danby'," Uncle Guido said. "The only jerk who writes his name with pictures is illiterate."

"Exactly," I agreed. "He could also be a lost Egyptian who only wrote in tombs, but I doubt it. So let's go at this another way. What if it says, 'I rather bee?' Then the question is: I'd rather be what?"

We all stared at the pictograph on the wall for a long, silent minute.

Then the answer to the puzzle came to me in a nearly blinding flash and I announced, "The message, I believe, is 'I'd rather be skiing.' See, the eye stands for I, the Dan Rather cartoon means 'rather,' the bee is the letter 'B' and the stick figure on the skis stands for skiing. As Sherlock Holmes always said, 'Elementary, my dear Watson.' Someone entered this outhouse and carefully created a message telling anyone who followed him that he'd prefer frolicking in the snow than eliminating his waste here. So, the question is, what kind of a clue is that?"

"Damned if I know," Uncle Guido said, "But then who's going to leave a message in a shitter anyhow? I've never understood what kind of person puts phone numbers and poems on bathroom walls."

"Well, if it was written by our serial killer," I theorized, "It means that he is crazier and more clever than we thought."

Pro asked, "How you figure that?"

"Crazier because he draws pictures on bathroom walls. More clever because the message he leaves doesn't help us in the slightest," I said. "It's as if he's mocking us."

"Get real," Pro said. "Some turds-for-brains put this up while he was jagging off to a picture of Brittany Spears or something like that."

I had to give the man credit, "You may be right. But you also might be wrong."

"And you," my Uncle Guido said, "Got your head up your ass on this thing. We're going to follow up one of my leads next."

Chapter Seven

In the limousine on the way to Chicago, Uncle Guido explained why he thought I was barking up the wrong tree, consulting the incorrect tea leaves and humping a wooden leg.

"Listen and listen good," he said in his most serious tone of voice. "Your father doesn't even know this story because the family never completely trusted your dad. Your mother was never allowed to know because no Testosteroni blood ran in her veins, which was a good thing since she married your father. Otherwise, you might have been born a lemon head or with six fingers and toes or whatever."

"Don't you have six toes Uncle Guido?"

"Keep your nose out of my toes, Tony, in more ways than one if you understand my meaning."

I did.

Uncle Guido continued, "You, we trust, so far. Kapeesh?"

Anxious to hear Uncle Guido's family story, I said, "Kapeesh," and with that I was accepted into the innest-in-group of my family. I was so far "In" that the group might very well have consisted of only my Uncle Guido and me. I was so very proud of that.

According to my Uncle Guido the secret, sworn enemies of the entire Testosteroni family are the Scrotaris. The Scrotaris have been the source of everything bad that has happened to the Testosteronis since the beginning of time.

Centuries ago, if a Testosteroni stubbed his or her toe, they would curse, "Tripped by a damned Scrotari again."

Uncle Guido reminded me that, when I was going out for the high school football team, I went out for a long pass. If I'd caught it, I would have made the team. But I didn't.

Uncle Guido asked me, "Who blind-sided you, knocked you flat on your ass, causing you to twist your knee and end your dreams of playing football? A Scrotari, that's who."

I couldn't deny that possibility because I'd never seen the guy who hit me and knocked me unconscious.

Uncle Guido asked me if I remembered my Uncle Jerome, who always married women who hated him and took all his money?

Of course I remembered Uncle Jerome. It was said of him that, rather than getting married, he would have been much better off just going up to a complete stranger every five years and give her his house. According to Uncle Guido, it was later learned that all of those women were secret Scrotaris, who had changed their names and hidden their identities so they could make just one Testosteroni miserable.

"Jerome," Uncle Guido sadly said, "was gang Scrotaried."

He revealed that the beginning of the troubles between our two families went all the way back to a wedding gift that was not delivered to poor Maria Testosteroni in the 13th century.

Uncle Guido ominously said, "And what makes the insult even worse is that Maria was a Scrotari on her mother's side. When she married one of us, those gorgonzola gophers immediately hated her, their own flesh. And that's why no Scrotari has been invited to a Testosteroni wedding since 1226 a. D. And they won't be until one of them delivers a suitable wedding present to the grave of the bride."

I made the mistake of asking, "But who cares? The bride and the groom and everyone who might have attended the wedding have been dead for eight centuries. Isn't it time to let bygones be bygones?"

"The last time I visited the grave of Maria Testosteroni, who died of a broken heart in 1247," Uncle Guido said, as his voice began to crack, "I asked myself: did someone leave a present there? Could bygones be bygones? Oh, no. The only thing on that grave was a little dog shit. Dog shit. Another Scrotari insult. It's the only thing they're good at."

Uncle Guido told me he wanted to call on some Scrotaris to see if they had anything to do with the two bodies found in my parents' living room and he'd like me to go with him.

"But," he warned, "Tony, you got to learn to shut up, keep your ears open and your farts to yourself. Think you can do that?"

I readily agreed, although I feared that this quest would take me far afield from solving the two murders and learning why Chad Parkington suddenly loved bad movies. It would also further delay the day when I could put the blocks to the beautiful Amanda. But this was family and I could not say no.

As Pro drove us to Chicago, Uncle Guido continued to tell me about the Scrotaris, who seemed to be a family whose every waking hour was devoted to destroying my family.

He said, "They breed like rabbits. All the Scrotari women get pregnant the first time they have sex and don't stop until they have a dozen kids. Don't even look cross-eyed at a Scrotari woman--they get knocked up that easily. They figure if they can't fight us, they can out-breed us and destroy our family essence by inter-breeding with us."

Pro added, "They stink."

129

"You see, Pro knows," my Uncle Guido said. "Not only that, but the men wear their pants so low that you can always see the cracks of asses. It's one of the sure-fire ways of identifying a Scrotari."

They sounded like awful people to me. But Uncle Guido's description also resembled the attributes given to any group that was the subject of prejudice. When whites think about blacks and vice versa, when Latinos consider whites and vice versa, and probably when Greenlanders think about Icelanders. The "other" group is often seen through a filter of prejudice. Although I am enlightened beyond the powers of most ordinary people, I'm not immune.

When I think of ordinary cops, I think they eat doughnuts too fast. When I think of anyone still employed in the dot com world, I know that they lie, cheat and would steal their own grandma's false teeth if given the chance. It's almost impossible not to view the world through the prism of prejudice

(Note to self: "prism of prejudice" is a good phrase. Use it again somewhere else.)

Since it would be impossible on such short notice to change Uncle Guido's attitude, and since I didn't know if what he was saying was true or not, I went along with his observations to prevent any tension between us.

By way of offering the least disagreement with him that I could, I said, "Right, we ought to tear their balls off and feed them to the pigs after cooking them in a light mornay sauce."

"That's my nephew," Uncle Guido proudly said. "Testosteroni blood runs deep in your veins. I told your father when he was 20 years old that the Scrotaris smelled bad—it was the only part of the story he ever knew--he wanted to buy some soap and offer it to them whenever we met so they'd smell better."

Pro snorted, "Stupido."

130

Uncle Guido warned, "Hey, that's the boy's father you're talking about, Pro. Let's just say your dad was misguided when he was your age."

We stopped in front of what appeared to be a dance hall called the Have a Ball Club.

A half a dozen tough-looking young men with their pants seemingly held in place by their asses and pubic hairs lounged around the entrance.

When the three of us got out of the car, all the men went on alert. It was even more ominous that the women who were hanging out with them suddenly disappeared into the entrance of the club.

Uncle Guido shouted in a commanding voice, "Anyone makes a move towards us and you'll understand the meaning of my motto: the only good Scrotari is a dead Scrotari."

The men grumbled amongst themselves for a few seconds and then opened a path for us to enter the Have a Ball club. Inside, in blazing lights, I could see the club's slogan "Where your balls have a ball."

As the three of us walked to the center of the dance floor, the throbbing jungle rhythm of the one man band's drum machine suddenly slowed and then went silent. The patrons were closing the path behind us as we walked deeper into the hall.

Uncle Guido whispered, "Don't worry. One Testosteroni is worth a hundred of these stupid creapolas."

As we entered the hall, I saw a beautiful brunet standing nearly in our path. She had flashing brown eyes, fabulous breasts, long legs, hair that tumbled down around her shoulders, inviting lips and the hips of love.

"Hello," I said, stopping in front of her as Uncle Guido plunged forward. "My name is Tony."

"And my name is Maria," she said, with a slight toss of her curls, laughter in her voice and an invitation in her eyes.

"Would you like to dance?" I asked, "And later come to my place for some serious fooling around with matrimony a future possibility." Then I remembered my uncle's warning about Scrotari fertility, so I quickly added, "Only kidding."

Her hand reached out to mine when a young man grabbed it and pulled her away. "No Testosteroni is going to touch my sister," he said and he tried to spit at me. His huge hocker missed and hit one of his own people.

Maria said, "That is my hot headed brother, Barnardo, the leader of what we call The Sharks."

I looked right at him and said, "I saw this movie when it was called 'West Side Story.' I went to the play when it was called 'Romeo and Juliet.' I've even heard about it when it was a Spanish musical called 'Don't Fuck With My Sister, Fredo.' Do you want to know what will happen?"

There was a difference of opinion. Some did, some didn't. They took a vote and by a 12-2 margin they asked me to predict the future for them.

"You hate me, I hate you, we're from rival gangs, but I love your sister and she loves me," I said.

"Over my dead body," Barnardo warned, but I ignored him.

I continued, "Sure, sure, that's what they all say. You dance in a threatening but faggy way. We dance, too. Then we sing about one kiss, Maria's best friend sings about life in America, everybody gets upset until Maria fakes her death. Then I kill myself and Maria really kills herself. And nobody lives happily ever after. You want a story like that? Or maybe we do a re-write for our generation, for our time. So you back off now; Maria learns that I cut my toenails in bed; I think she's imagining re-arranging the furniture while we're making love; we break up and everybody lives about the way they do now. So which story do you want?"

Before he could answer, I heard my Uncle Guido bellowing, "Any of you weasels man enough to admit to dumping bodies in my bother's house?"

132

Someone in the crowd shouted, "Whomever did that was not very tidy."

Another heckler in the crowd asked, "Why would we do that? We'd rather leave your dead body in a railroad washroom, Vincenzo the Bellicose."

Things got even more tense after that. Out of the corner of my eye, I could see that Maria's brother, Barnardo, was about to take a swing at me. My quick thinking saved the day.

I grabbed Maria and put her in front of me. Barnardo missed with first swing, but his second swing got her right in the breadbasket. I was lucky--if that punch had hit me in the stomach, it really would have hurt.

Maria fell to the floor shouting, "You have killed our baby, my brother."

Suddenly I had serious doubts about marrying in to that family. Would all our children look like Barnardo?

Then, with Uncle Guido and Pro at my side, all three of us began punching and kicking anyone in our path. It was actually a lot of fun for us. For them it might have been somewhat less entertaining.

We made it back through the entrance, got in our car and raced off, chased by two black SUVs full of Scrotaris.

Pro asked, "Why is this happening?"

I knew the answer was, "Because it is time. In every case solved by every detective since the beginning of investigative police work there has been a chase of some kind. Now is the time for ours."

We were driving down alleys, knocking over garbage cans, which flew into the windshields of the Scrotari SUVs.

We made turns on two wheels, narrowly avoiding women pushing baby carriages. We did not know why mothers were out with their babies at 2 A. M. but in this neighborhood there seemed to hundreds of mothers with babies always directly in our path.

As Pro swerved to avoid them, he muttered, "God damn Scrotari."

Uncle Guido was shooting at our pursuers out of the back window. His shots caused one Scrotari SUV to turn towards a ramp that happened to be in the middle of the street down which we were chasing. Ramps frequently create obstacles during car chases and that seems to be their only function.

The Scrotari SUV canted over on two wheels, but the chase continued with Scrotari gunmen firing from the windows.

It was such a good stunt that I almost began applauding until I realized that the SUV contained Scrotaris who wanted to kill us.

The SUV on two wheels rolled into a barrel of some sort, which happened to be standing in the middle of the street. The barrel then exploded, sending up a ball of yellow and red flames three stories high.

Both pursuing SUVs ploughed through the wall of flames. The SUV on two wheels righted itself. With four wheels on the ground, it was able to close the distance between us.

This time I had no urge to applaud because that was something I had seen a dozen times before in the movies.

In any case, I didn't have much time to look at our pursuers because Pro took a left turn out of the alley and put the car into a four-wheel 360-degree spin.

Our tires squealed but didn't flatten and the noise we made wasn't heard by the Scrotaris chasing us--another result I expected after watching hundreds of car chase scenes in movies.

We stopped just out of sight of the entrance to an alley. Only a second or two later, the two Scrotari SUVs chasing us came barreling across the entrance to the alley. They didn't see or sense us until Pro gunned the motor.

Suddenly, our roles were reversed. Instead of them chasing us, we were chasing them. They were shooting back at us while Uncle Guido and I were firing forward at them. Pro was driving close enough to them to slam their rear bumpers, causing them to momentarily lose control.

I shouted, "Look, up ahead. There is an old man pushing a cart filled, oddly enough with a huge mound of vegetables and window panes."

There was, of course, no time to think why would a pushcart peddler was selling windows and produce at 2 A. M. in an alley in Chicago.

The Scrotari SUV ploughed into the cart, breaking every window and crushing every orange and cucumber.

Trying to avoid the now-destroyed cart, Pro slammed into another cart loaded with brassieres.

I know. It's hard to figure why a man should be walking down this street at that time of night pushing a cart filled with Victoria's Secret merchandise. It even occurred to me that, although push carts have not been popular in Chicago for nearly 40 years, on this night we sideswiped two of them in as many minutes.

The last crash into a pushcart caused problems for Pro, who couldn't see because his window was covered with dozens of lacy bras.

I leaned out and tried to clear some away. I grabbed a few bras, kept one "for good luck" and offered one to Uncle Guido for his wife.

He politely said, "No thanks, but I will take one to give to my honey on the side. That's why you should join the organization. Once you're in, you automatically get a woman to fool around with. It's in the bylaws."

Sounded like a great organization.

When the windshield was cleared, the Scrotaris seemed to have vanished like a bad red wine stain after you put on club soda and salt.

(Note to reader: other books offer recipes as an inducement for you to buy them. Among its other advantages, my book reveals the secret of getting rid of wine stains. You may not be much of a cook, but in this lifetime, as certainly as a Chicago Cubs hitter fouling out with the bases loaded in the bottom of the ninth, red wine will almost certainly stain something you own.)

My Uncle Guido put the capper on the entire experience by asking and answering a rhetorical question, "What did we learn from this? Drive faster and we'd have caught the motherfuckers.

Chapter Eight

Our foray into the Scrotari camp that ended with our exit in a blazing blizzard of bras meant that I could proceed with my own investigations in good conscience. I had done my best to uphold the family honor.

The next day it was raining with light sheets of mist coming down like curtains after the last act of a play about talking vaginas.

(I put that in because weather is very important in almost any detective's life. I think it sets the mood, deepens the suspense and makes the book longer.

(The foremost practitioner of the weather-as-plot school of detecting is Dave Robicheaux, who works in the swamp country of Louisiana, where it rains so much the alligators are water-logged. The thunder and the climactic conditions of the swamp exactly match Robicheaux's moods and predict where the quest will lead him.)

That day, the light rain became a torrential downpour resembling the tears of a virgin who discovers that her chosen deflowerer is penis deficient. At that point, my first stop was Don D'Wangle, agent and matchmaker for Chad and Freedom.

I had heard a lot about Don over the years and none of the stories were good. As an agent, he demanded 15 per cent of everything, although D'Wangle has strenuously denied that his cut included 15 per cent of all his client's conjugal visits. He did admit that he partook of a client's wife's favors once when they were a Christmas present from a particularly satisfied client. D'Wangle reportedly said, "She was so wonderful in bed, I considered upping my fee to 20 per cent."

He has called himself "Your agent for life," meaning that whether a client is on the way up or at the sad and slippery bottom of a career, D'Wangle will continue to take his cut. D'Wangle successfully filed a law suit that forced one long-time client, who was down on his luck and living in a skid row flophouse, to turn over 15 per cent of the food he got in the Salvation Army soup kitchen.

D'Wangle has represented television anchormen, including one who was functionally blind. Nonetheless, the client got a lucrative contract because of the nickname D'Wangle created for him. Even a blind "Stud Muffin" was worth $550,000 a year.

D'Wangle also got large contracts and bonuses for Chicago Cub players who could not hit, field or pitch. He convinced the Chicago Tribune, owners of the Chicago Cubs, that the players D'Wangle represented were vital to continuing the century-long Cub tradition of having losing seasons. D'Wangle pushed his demands a little too far when he demanded a bonus every time his batters struck out or his pitchers lost a game.

D'Wangle's office was festooned with pictures of the agent shaking hands with his clients and friends. Glossy photos were said to be removed from D'Wangle's walls the moment any of his clients are indicted.

D'Wangle was one of those fat men who give obesity a bad name. From his slimy hair to his fingertips and presumably down to his toes, D'Wangle exuded grease.

When he raised his palms off the blotter on his desk to shake my hand when I entered his office, the handprints remained on the blotter like an oil stain beneath a 1957 Ford that needed new shaft seals since it was used to run moonshine on the backroads of Kentucky.

138

And when we shook, our hands slipped back and forth like a love piston in the well-oiled tunnel of a two-bit whore on the first Saturday night after the fleet has docked in Honolulu.

It was said that talking to Don D'Wangle was like conversing with a black widow spider with PMS and a bad attitude. He was so powerful and completely ruthless that I shuddered involuntarily when he asked, "What can I do you for?"

"I understand your client Chad P. has gone soft in his movie reviews," I said, attempting to sneer and look tough. I may have only succeeded in looking vaguely nauseous.

"Soft shmoft, hard shmard," D'Wangle replied.

It would be weeks before I realized that was the way he dismissed anyone who questioned him or his clients.

I was silly enough to ask the great agent, "What do you mean 'soft shmoft, hard shmard'? Is that some sort of code? Is this some arcane revelation that means there will be a decline in network TV ratings in 2009?"

D'Wangle answered, "None of the above. It's just the secret of sounding like you're talking Yiddish. You add a "Sh" in front of the word."

"But why would you want to fake speaking Yiddish?" I asked.

"Fake shmake," D'Wangle said, so I immediately answered, "Yiddish shmiddush."

"I think he's got it," D'Wangle enthused, "By George, I think he's got it."

I said, "Got it, sh-mot it" and D'Wangle asked, "What kind of monster have I created? All right, what do you want? I can only give you 10 seconds of my valuable time."

"I want to know," I began.

I was interrupted by D'Wangle, "Time's up. No hard feelings. I'm a very busy man."

"None," I said, oozing with charm, "If you think you can tell me why Chad P. suddenly loves every crap movie that comes down the pike?"

"Sonny boy, it's been going around," D'Wangle said. "Clarence Coward III, theater critic for the New York Times, just wrote a 'reconsideration' of 'Cats' and called that piece of dreck the 'apotheosis of the American musical.' According to Clarence, 'Memories' is the finest song since King David wrote 'The Song of Psalms' in the Bible."

I responded, "I kind of like humans dressed as sexy kittens."

"Yes, but no other serious theater critic has liked 'Cats' in the last two decades," D'Wangle said. "Then there was Dean Dempsey, television critic for the Los Angeles Times, who wrote that we're entering a new Golden Age of TV and that 'Who Wants to Be a Millionaire' had more drama per second than 'Marty' ever did. Dempsey also threatened to 'vote off the island anyone in the world who didn't love Survivor.'"

"But," I persisted, "Who would benefit if the critics changed their stripes?"

"Wouldn't make any no never mind to me," D'Wangle claimed. "I get my 15 per cent as long as the client continues to breathe and, in the case of residuals, well after they've rotted to nothing but bones."

"You're all heart, D'Wangle," I said.

He winked, "Look, a good agent doesn't need to dance down the yellow brick road and try to meet the wizard."

"Come again?" I said.

"Because we have no need of a heart. Get it?" D'Wangle explained. "Anyway, who's Chad gonna hurt? Producers don't care as long as the public continues watching Three Guys at the Movies. The public will continue to go to their favorite movies, watch television shows or attend musicals no matter what the critics say. The only people who care about what the critics say are the actors and even then it's only important to the struggling actors."

"So, are you saying I should look for a struggling actor who doesn't like the critics?" I asked.

When he nodded in agreement, I thanked him for that insight and said, "So long, shmo long."

He answered, "Get outa here, shmet outa here."

As I left, he flicked his hands at me and large grease spots appeared on the back of my fake camel's-hair sports coat, something I did not know until I got to my parents home, took it off and realized it looked like the bottom of the cardboard container for a cheap pizza. I sent D'Wangle the cleaning bill, which he has never paid.

The perceptive reader will notice that I did not reveal to D'Wangle that Chad had disappeared. I had two reasons for maintaining my discretion: (1) a good detective keeps his mouth shut and doesn't share really big secrets even with his own mother, (2) he'd probably say it didn't make any difference as long as he got his 15 per cent.

Wait, I just remembered I actually had three reasons why I never told D'Wangle that Chad was among the missing. Number three was: (3) I completely forgot to bring it up.

I was a little disappointed that during our meeting, D'Wangle didn't try to wangle a representation contract with me. He was supposed to do that with almost everyone else. Why not me?

After thinking about it, I concluded I was probably too tough for him to handle. I'd hate to have to slap him around while we were negotiating. And a .45 slug between his greasy eyes might seriously affect our client/agent relationship.

My next stop was a face-to-face with Amanda, who had hired me to find out about Chad. I needed to fill her in on what I had learned about Chad's change of heart and subsequent disappearance. Hopefully, our face-to-face would lead to a cheek-to-cheek (either facially or butt-illy), which would segue into a humpety-to-humpety including a sampling of her oral talents.

I found her at the television studio where Three Guys at the Movies was being taped. They were in the midst of completing a segment.

Trey Parker, who looked as if he'd gained the equivalent of an additional human being since their show last week, was overflowing one couch which looked strained to the point of imminent collapse. Parker was yelling that movies with scenes and cuts were beneath contempt. Again espousing his unfathomable "Naturalistische Film Making" theory, Parker was saying that what was most wrong about film were the names "movies" and "motion pictures" because they implied movement. He shouted, "Actors move, cameras stay still," which was greeted with hoots of contempt from his fellow panelists.

Parker was not deterred and he vowed, "I will not like any film until all cameras are locked down in concrete."

Freddie Niles, more gnomish and uglier than ever, sneared, "You're the one that should be locked down in concrete, preferably head—and mouth—first."

Niles sulked in his leather seat, from which he glowered at everyone in the studio. His face was so full of hate that he seemed to be yearning to immediately use a weapon of mass destruction.

During my visit, a small boy walked through the studio holding his daddy's hand. The kid took one look at Niles and began screaming, "That Troll wants to eat me alive." Although his father quickly took the boy out of the studio, the kid's comment put Niles in an even worse mood. Niles began muttering, "Parker, anyone with your opinions deserves the slow-death penalty." It seemed to me that this was hardly the give-and-take that the producers wanted.

A small person, possibly a dwarf, sat silently in the third seat. This person wore what looked like a blue pillow case over his entire head. The short, bagged person would nod in the direction of anyone who was speaking.

When Parker stopped to take a breath, Chad's voice could be heard over the studio's loud speakers. He was viciously criticizing the movie under discussion, calling it "garbage," "sewage of the mind" and "a waste of time and money." He also attacked Parker, calling him a "pea brain atop a lard body." Chad added that Parker's theory of movie criticism was worth less than the sweat on a weightlifter's crotch.

Chad continued his personal attacks by accusing Niles of sniffing crotchless panties during the last seven movie screenings. He said, "Freddie, you're so ugly the doctors tried to put you back in your mother's womb after you were born."

All in all, it was vintage Three Guys at the Movies. While keeping an eye on the segment being taped, I glance up at the in-studio monitors. On the screen, there was a close-up of the Chad in a bag, only the bag wasn't there. Instead, Chad's face could be seen talking as if he had never disappeared at all.

When I noticed Amanda standing towards the back of the studio, I sidled over to her and said, "Animatronic? Like Lincoln endlessly reciting the Gettysburg address in some museum or historical society?"

"Oh, it's much better than that," Amanda said and she signaled me to follow her outside. In the hallway, she explained in a whisper, "Breathe a word of this and I'll have you killed."

"Cross my heart and hope not to die," I promised.

Amanda impatiently exhaled. Apparently after looking at my face and noticing my insouciant expression of feigned interest, she evidently deciding that I was trustworthy. Or perhaps she decided that, if I did tell anyone what she was about to reveal, she could go back to kicking my balls through the goalposts of my ass cheeks.

For whatever the reasons, she continued, "Without his permission, while he was with the show, we digitally sampled Chad. Now, because we own his image, we can have him say anything we want. In fact, we're finding that the taping goes much more smoothly without Chad's interference. His image never storms off the set and stays in his dressing room because of some imaginary slight. Now he doesn't have to go to the bathroom for three hours."

I found that curious, "He would do that?"

"Sometimes longer," Amanda said. "No one could figure out why although we suspected that he was hanging himself from the towel bars in an effort to grow tall."

I felt sorry for him and said, "The poor little guy."

"You only feel that way because you have never worked with him," Amanda snapped. "Before he conveniently disappeared, Chad was usually a little asshole. Now he's quite easy to get along with, a dream panelist."

Politely avoiding any comment on her "little asshole" phrase as it might apply to a dwarf, I interrupted, "My investigation indicates that Chad was the victim of a serial killer."

"Chad is dead?" she asked.

"Not that we know of," I answered. "At this point we have not found his body."

"Then why do you think a serial killer is involved?"

"Good question," I said. "I believe that maybe the perp is just not very good at being a serial killer. He could be just learning." I was happy to be able to work in technical detecting terms like "perp" whenever I could. For those of you not familiar with the term, a "perp" is someone who perplexes the detective. Whenever a detective in movies, on TV, in books or real life uses the term "perp", he or she is indicating that they are "perplexed" or confused about who

144

did the crime. Once you know this, you'll be able to understand a lot more about the films you see and books you read.

"All that is theoretical right now," Amanda said, "Frankly, we need Chad even less today than we did when he was with the show."

Something about this was disquieting. "You said when Chad 'was' with the show. Does that mean he's been fired in his absence?"

"Hardly," she scoffed. "It means we do not need him anymore. Sure, we'll pay him a stipend for the use of his image for a little while until the next budget-cutting exercise. No, you're the one that's fired. If we don't need him, we certainly don't need you to find him."

"But... but...but." I sounded like a motorboat running out of gas as it drifted into the shoals of depression on the stream of annoyance in the current of despair.

"Does this mean you and I are never going out and you'll never..." I simply ran out of words to express my overwhelming feelings. I was reduced to the following pantomime: I pointed to my crotch, I pointed to my mouth and I shoved my index finger in and out of my mouth. While doing that, I looked at her with the pleading expression of a dog that needs to go out but is being ignored while its owner talks on the phone to a girlfriend who now doesn't want anything to do with him.

Amanda turned on her heels and walked away. I was devastated, I was upset, and I was left with no one to talk to. However, like so many detectives, I was perfectly able to have an excellent internal dialogue with myself at any time.

I thought, "It is well known that once someone is a client of any tough, hard-bitten detective, that person remains a client forever. This applies after the death of the client. The hardened detective keeps on detecting even if he's been lied to or cheated out of money that is owed him. The detective looks for the murderer no matter how many times the dick is beaten, jailed or threatened. Nor does he care who he hurts in that quest. Often, the real murderer is the person who hired the detective in the first place and that reinforces the good gumshoe's notion that everyone lies, cheats, steals and murders. At that point, the shamus once again knows that one is to be trusted, not even the detective who usually lies to himself about the little things like love and friendship. And that's why I can't give up...and I'm not going to!!"

(Insert applause here or a scene of the detective's friends patting him on the back in congratulations. If you are reading this alone and no one is looking, it is all right to pat yourself on the back. Right now.)

It was as fine an internal dialogue as I'd ever had with myself. Not once did I interrupt my train of thought with my normal admonitions of, "You are dumber than a box of rocks" or "You're giving stupid people bad names again" or thoughts to that effect.

That was when they grabbed me. I had just left the television studio and was walking along, minding my own business, when out of a blue colored sky, wham!, bam!, no, thank you, ma'am, I was grabbed from behind. Something that smelled like a horse blanket was thrown over my head, my arms were tied to my sides, and I was kicked into the back seat of a car, which immediately sped away.

From within the blanket, I protested, "But I didn't call for a taxi. And even if I did, this is no way to treat a potential fare."

Someone slammed what felt like an elbow into the top of my head and said, "Shut the fuck up."

OK, so now I understood what was expected of me.

After about a half-hour's drive, the car stopped. I was roughly grabbed under both armpits and hoisted out of the car to a standing position. Whoever was kidnapping me didn't even bother to make sure that my head cleared the top of the door. Didn't these people ever watch TV reality

146

shows like "Cops"? Even if you hate the guy you've grabbed, you protect his head as he's going in or out of a car. It is simply the way these things are done. I promised myself that I'd write an angry letter to someone when this was all over.

I was pushed and prodded forward until I was forced to sit. Then I was tied to the chair and the blanket was taken off of me.

I was in a small room. The only furniture was a large-screen television set that had the fuzzy picture that indicated it was waiting for videotape to be played.

A tall, well-dressed man entered the room. Standing before me, looking as handsome as he was when he played Husker Smith, the arch villain of the soap opera "Lives of Fulfillment," was Tremayne, the actor with no last name. There was once a rumor that he foreswear having a last name because his actual first name was Forgettable. It didn't matter because the critics usually referred to him as Forgettable Tremayne anyway.

His voice was low and threatening, he was scowling and appeared quite angry. As with most of his acting appearances, Tremayne's attention seemed to be split between the line he was delivering and his oh so pleased observation of himself at work. He seemed to be the phoniest person in this room and there were only two of us there.

Tremayne said, "You have been quite bothersome to us."

I suggested, "Let's take that line again and this time do it with some feeling."

That was when he slapped me hard across the face. He did it without a hint of phoniness. It was then that I decided to batten down the wise guy act in favor of survival.

"Since you won't remember anything that happens here," Tremayne sneered, "I might as well boast to you of our accomplishments."

"So you're like the babbling bad guy in the movies," I observed. "The one who always talks too much to the hero just before the good guy frees himself and beats the crap out of the bad guys."

"Except this time, evil wins," Tremayne said. "We have found that repeated screenings of movies that resonate with a subject's soul can produce profound changes. Chad had to watch two full weeks of round-the-clock showings of 'The Sound Of Music' before he emerged as a much better person and a more positive-minded movie critic. We estimate that after a mere two days of 'Hudson Hawk,' you will become an even more senseless wretch than you now are."

The full horror of what he planned to do slowly dawned upon me. He and his group had discovered that bad movies judiciously applied could produce brainwashing of a scope far greater than ever imagined in the Soviet Union, North Korea or commercials for Disney cruises.

It was diabolical. It was mean. And it might just drive me crazy. And it might kill me. I immediately wondered if I would prefer death to multiple viewings of "Hudson Hawk." And I thought I might.

But I also knew I was still on the job, despite being fired by Amanda so I demanded, "What did you do with Chad Parkington?"

"You hardly have the right to ask anything of me, but I'm going to tell you anyway," Tremayne said. "Chad was our first experimental subject and we went a little too far. Large parts of his personality were stripped away in addition to his critical perceptions. We figured that someone might notice the change, put two and two together. Also we were 10 days late in bringing 'The Sound Of Music' back to Blockbuster. They do keep records of that sort of thing -- and that might endanger this operation. So we sent him away."

"You'll never get away with this," I said. "If you do this to me, I'll get you if it is the last thing I ever do."

148

After 10 seconds of exceedingly annoying, phony snickers, Tremayne said, "We have already gotten away with this again and again. With a television critic who began praising the drama of shopping channels when he returned to work after being subjected to only 20 minutes of Robert Stack introductions. With an art critic, who softened after being forced to stare at the thatched homes with twinkling lights painted by Thomas Kinkade for only seven minutes. And, with your own father after forcing him to watch only two Susanne Sommers thigh cruncher commercials."

I began to struggle against the ropes while I shouted, "You bastard. That's why dad enjoys watching her so much that he hasn't given my mother marital comfort for years. Well, come to think of it, he didn't give her much comfort before the commercials began to run. I'll tear your thighs out when I get free."

Tremayne, still snickering, threatened, "When we're done with you, you'll barely remember your own name, let alone any vendetta you might have against me."

Tremayne suddenly changed his emotional tone and got very serious, "Do you have any last thoughts before all your thoughts are permanently erased?"

"Yes, one thing," I said as I was determined not to go quietly into that thoughtless night. "You are a big doo-doo head."

After proving that I could give as well as I could take it, I asked, "Why are you doing this?"

"World domination, of course,' Tremayne said and then he laughed. "Ha ha ha, just joking—but perhaps not. I mean, if we can get a critic to alter his or her opinions, why not a judge? Or clerks for home owners' insurance policies who decide that a broken appliance is not covered. Or referees and umpires. What about CEOs and middle managers, who decide whom to fire. We'd like to get to the people who set up those telephone answering trees that always begin 'listen closely because our menu has changed.' In fact, we could affect anyone who makes a decision. Come to think of it, it could result in world domination."

"You are mad," I said. "Are you working alone?"

"No, and that's the beauty part," Tremayne answered. "Our organization right now is small, consisting of the few actors around Sears Point who have ever gotten a bad review. In smaller, regional theaters you really have to stink or have screwed the critic's girlfriend to get a negative review. In the future, we'll be joined by anyone who has ever gotten a bad notice, a bad rating on an employment evaluation, or even a negative reaction on a date. We'll be huge."

With that, Tremayne started the video of "Hudson Hawk." If you remember, this was the story of a robber, played by Bruce Willis, who knew the exact time length of songs in their standard arrangements. Willis sang while opening safes so he could time how long he could stay in the museum he was burgling. It was not the most brilliant plot ever foisted on an unsuspecting public by Hollywood.

Once "Swinging on a Star" was over, Willis should have burgled and beat it. When I saw the movie the first time and Willis asked the musical question "Or would you rather be a mule?", I remember shouting, "Anything, anywhere but being in this theater watching you."

During my first viewing as an unwilling patron, when Bruce Willis began singing "Big Girls Don't Cry-Ay-Ay," I began to whimper myself.

"Please," I said, "This is cruel and unusual punishment."

"Ha ha," Tremayne laughed. "Wait until you've seen it two dozen times. And don't try to shut your eyes—we have toothpicks to handle that. Or we could permanently glue your eyelashes to your eyebrows, forcing you to go through life looking like a rabbit caught in the headlights. Either way is not pleasant. We're betting that after the second viewing, you can sing either 'The Hokey Pokey' or 'The Name Game' better than Bruce Willis could."

Before Tremayne finished his little speech, the video had rewound and "Hudson Hawke" began again.

I got angry when I realized that (1) I was losing my mind, (2) a mind, even my mind, is a terrible thing to lose, (3) I should have put the newspaper delivery on vacation hold before I came here, and (4) this also happened to little Chad.

Tremayne returned after the third screening. He asked, "How are we doing?"

I answered, "If you hate to go to school, you may grow up to be a mule."

"You're progressing nicely," he observed. "If I let you go right now, what would you do to me?"

"You'd be better off than you are," I answered, "You could be swingin' on a star."

"Twenty five more screenings should do the trick," Tremayne said. "After that, you'd rather be a pig."

He laughed again. I wondered if it was justifiable homicide to kill someone for having a phony, maniacal laugh of a demented mule.

Tremayne hit the "play" button for another screening of a movie, which would never carry moonbeams home in a jar, when the door to the room burst open. Standing there, silhouetted in the brilliant sunlight, was my cavalry, my rescuers: my Uncle Guido and Pro.

Pro, after looking at the opening titles for "Hudson Hawk," observed, "They put Surgeon General's warnings on cigarettes, but not on crap like this."

"Oh, Pro," I said, "All the monkeys aren't in the zoo."

Uncle Guido whispered to Pro, "I hope we're not too late. He might have lost all his intelligence."

151

Pro quietly speaks in Uncle Guido's ear, "With all do respect, boss, how would you know?"

"Can't you see?" Uncle Guido protested. "My nephew sounds like an idiot."

Pro whispered back, "Observation noted, but then it's not all that much of a change, is it boss?"

With that, they began swinging punches at Tremayne, who threw up his hands and shrieked, "Not in the face. It's my fortune."

Pro popped him a good left jab in the nose and pointed out, "I thought there's always more jobs for guys who look a little used up."

"But I'd have to go through the expense of getting new publicity pictures," complained Tremayne as he whiffed a big roundhouse punch at Pro.

That's when two other guys came running into the room. I recognized one as the actor who had become the face of hemorrhoids on a television commercial. His line was, "Relief is only a rub-a-dub-dub away." I thought I recognized the other guy as the skinny man, naked except for his black socks, who brings in the towels at the end of the action in porno movies, but I wasn't sure.

They ran forward to threaten Pro and Uncle Guido, who put up a huge hand, stopping them in their tracks. My uncle asked, "You guys actors?"

They agreed, so Uncle Guido asked, "What role you acting now? The tough guys? Bad casting, because you're acting and I'm not."

With that, Uncle Guido punched both of them in the stomach, picked them up by their collars, slammed their heads together so hard I could almost hear the birdies sing, and threw them out of the room.

Pro, meanwhile, was punching Tremayne in the mouth, while advising him, "A good right to the mouth beats collagen injections any day of the week."

152

Tremayne, who suddenly found himself sitting on the floor, raised his hands, signaling an end to the one-sided fight. He wheezed, "Much as I should appreciate your efforts to re-arrange my nose and add to my lips, I prefer a more standard cosmetic surgery approach, thank you."

"No problem," said Pro. "Just stay away from Tony here."

While Uncle Guido untied me, I shared the story of what happened to Chad. "Tremayne told me," I said, "that the little guy had been 'sent away'. I'm not sure exactly where."

Uncle Guido said, "Wait, there's a big FedEx box in front of the apartment. Could Chad be...?"

That was all Uncle Guido needed to say. Almost before Pro could complete his warning to Tremayne, "You stay put," we were standing in the hallway looking at a huge FedEx box. It was liberally festooned with labels saying "Undeliverable," "Noxious odors," "Leaking Contents," and "Return to Sender."

The label said that the box was supposed to be sent to Terra Del Fuego. The awful smell surrounding the box confirmed why FedEx did not accept it. The puddle on the rug around the box testified to another undeliverable aspect of the container.

From inside the box we could hear music and it sounded like someone was singing "Cream colored ponies and crisp apple strudels."

Pro took out his switchblade and quickly opened the box.

As the light from the hallway and the television cameras illuminated the interior of the box, Chad Parkington shut his eyes and winced. In his tiny lap, a portable VCR continued to play "The Sound of Music."

Before we could reach in and pull the little guy out, Freedom Plenty rushed forward, elbowing me, Uncle Guido and Pro out of the way. Freedom picked up Chad, holding the little guy off the floor and bringing him to her eye level. She hugged Chad and covered him with tearful kisses as three TV cameramen, who had suddenly materialized on the scene, recorded the tender reunion.

Uncle Guido whispered an explanation, "She called and insisted on coming along. Something about a sweeps piece promoting her show. Reunions are always good for ratings, Freedom said."

Freedom was purring, "My poor baby, I've missed you. Are you all right?"

All Chad could say as he nestled in the considerable mounds of Freedom's breasts was, "The hills are alive with the sound of music."

As they hugged, Freedom said, "I've learned that parting is such sweet sorrow, that tomorrow is emptier if you are not with me today, that being together is far better than being apart. And I'd want my viewers to know that love comes in all sizes and that the appearance of the package sometimes does not reveal what is really inside." She brushed back a tear.

And she sounded as if she were thinking up every word at the moment she spoke it rather than reading them off cue cards held by a young woman standing just outside camera range.

Chad smiled and asked, "Did you know that these are 'My Favorite Things'? I really like crisp apple strudel and schnitzel with noodles. Could you get me some for a snack, especially if they were spiced by whiskers on kittens?"

"I could, I could," cried Freedom. "And I will, just for you," after which she paused and looked meaningfully at the camera. She added, "...and for me."

Chad leaned closer to Freedom and then he advised her, "You know you should follow every rainbow till...you...find...your dream!"

What a moment. It was so real and so emotional that I didn't know if I should cry or applaud wildly. I did both. Unfortunately, that was probably not the sound that Freedom was going for during this tender reunion.

Freedom immediately shouted, "Cut. That wraps it, people. We need to get back to the studio. Pronto. Move it, move it."

Dropping poor Chad back into the box, Freedom said, "Clean yourself up, Chad. You're disgusting." Then she walked away.

I asked, "What does she expect of a guy locked into a FedEx cardboard box for two weeks without a toilet? Of course he smells shitty. Wouldn't you?"

Pro and Uncle Guido readily agreed, with Uncle Guido adding, "I think we ought to hose him down real good before we mention this to anyone else."

The three of us agreed. Chad was oblivious to any discussion because he preferred to stare at the tiny TV screen in front of him. Once more the hills were alive with the sound of mucous.

After the police took away Tremayne and began a search for his two actor associates, we got some clothes for Chad from a nearby children's clothing store and took the VCR away from him (no easy task because he was emotionally attached to it). We had to dispose of his FedEx box/home in a distant dumpster because people in rooms adjoining Tremayne's were complaining of the smell.

Only then were we able to talk about the successful conclusion of the case of the missing Chad. As we sauntered back to my parents' home, I asked Uncle Guido, "How did you find me?"

"A good citizen came to the brilliant conclusion that throwing a blanket over someone in broad daylight was a suspicious activity," Uncle Guido said.

Pro proudly added, "Don't let your Uncle Guido kid you. It was because of good legwork. When we begin asking questions of everyone we can find, we do tend to get answers. Or else. You know, your Uncle Guido woulda made a good cop."

"That's all I need—a sidekick with a potty mouth," Uncle Guido said, but I could tell he was almost proud of the compliment. "Why'd they put the little guy in a big box?"

"They explained that to me," I said. "They thought that too many viewings of 'The Sound Of Music' would drive Chad crazy and make him so stupid that people would notice the change and begin to ask questions."

Pro opined, "It might also have made him fall for little girls with pigtails who like to run over the hills of Germany or wherever."

"They were going to do the same to me," I said. "Thanks for saving my brains."

Uncle Guido said, "I think we were in time. I can hardly notice any difference."

I paused for a moment, gave my best Bruce Willis smirk, and then began singing "Would You Like To Swing On A Star?" I couldn't help myself. Anyway, that night all three of us were carrying figurative moonbeams home in a jar.

Chapter Nine

That night after a small celebration I told Uncle Guido and Pro how we would solve the remaining case involving the two almost-naked bodies found in my parents' living room.

It's the oldest method in the detective books," I said. "We gather all the suspects in one room. I question them, dazzle them with my brilliance and then the real murderer reveals himself. It happens all the time."

Uncle Guido had his doubts, "With the number of suspects we have right now, we'd be lucky to bring them all together on one continent, let alone in one room."

Pro added, "I hope we're not expected to serve them any snacks. That many pigs in a blanket could get expensive."

"I could cull the invitation list to, say, the most likely 10 or 20," I answered. "With everyone in the room, I reveal all the evidence against each person. We listen to their excuses and evasions. While they are talking, I stare at them like this..."

Uncle Guido observed, "Sort of like you just ate a Caesar salad with some bad anchovies?"

"Not exactly," I said. "It's the stare that burns through to the soul, I'm told."

Pro looked me in the eye and said, "I don't know. It kind of looks like you need to go to the bathroom or something."

"Har-de-har-har," I offered sarcastically. "OK, so I work on the stare. After the questioning, the evidence and the stare, someone usually confesses or does something suspicious, like pulling a gun or running from the room. Then we know."

"Worth a try," Uncle Guido said. "So what do we do next?"

"Defrost the bodies," I said. "Looking at dead bodies has been known to produce confessions."

"Not in my crowd," Uncle Guido said. "But maybe in yours."

The next few hours were a busy time. Getting Jerry Andrews out of my parents' freezer was no easy task. He was stiff, of course, and his flagstaff was even stiffer. Even if the guy was dead, we didn't want to break off the parental pole, as it were. That might lead to difficult questions from the police or the coroner.

With three of us working on him, it took over an hour to lift Jerry from the freezer. When we got him out, we noticed that a Swanson Frozen Turkey Dinner had been left in the freezer and was stuck to his back. Hopefully, the defrosting would cause it to fall off before an undertaker asked some questions more difficult than what is the proper microwave setting.

Thurmond Howarth, whose body was in the Clements freezer, was easier to remove because he had been in there a shorter amount of time. But getting him from the Clements house to my parents' home wasn't easy.

We walked alongside this six foot tall Popsicle, lifting him up so his feet would not scrape on the pavement. Except for the fact that he was wearing a muffler in July to conceal the strange shade of icy blue of his face, I thought everything looked fairly normal.

When we got him in the door of my parents' house, I said, "These guys should defrost in separate beds, otherwise they'll keep each other cold and slow down the process."

Uncle Guido agreed, so Pro took Thurmond to my parents' bed, while Jerry began to melt in my room.

Then the difficult work began – finding all the suspects and convincing them to gather in my parents' home. Merry Martha, who was a suspect because anyone involved with me could definitely be the murderer, happily accepted our invitation to my parents' home. Perhaps she thought she was going to be the beneficiary of a three-way involving me, Uncle Guido and Pro. Come to think of it, that was a definite possibility, especially if she brought her own salami in case we got the munchies afterwards.

I convinced Sheriff Clem to come over by hinting that I might be able to reveal the true identity of the person who sunk his boat three decades ago. OK, that was shameless and manipulative, but what can you expect of me? I'm a detective.

I wanted Freedom Plenty to be there even though she was certainly not a suspect. I hoped that she would see me at work, be impressed with my detecting skills, and invite me as a guest on her show. This appearance would lead to other guest shots, an offer to write a best-selling book and eventually my own talk show, the ultimate height of prestige in contemporary America. I left a message for her hinting that there was to be a meeting about a new diet that guaranteed a weight loss of more than 20 pounds a week.

Elmer Omittus, the electrician, was asked to drop by on the pretext that I needed an in-depth discussion of toilet back ups associated with septic field overloads—always something worth exploring in that damp part of Michigan.

I wanted Amanda, who was also not a suspect, to be there so she could see how competent I was. Then she might agree to a mad night of sex and lust with me.

Jim and Dottie Gerlund accepted my invitation after I told them that I owned a rare gaseous eggplant, which never bloomed. To attract flies which would pollinate the plant, I said that it "boomed" noxious odors. Actually, I'm rather proud of that story because, as whoppers go, I thought creating a farting eggplant was pretty clever.

The local grass cutter, George Svaboda, decided to visit my parents' home because we convinced him that we needed an emergency discussion about moles and dandelions.

Father Damian, who had wanted so much to examine Jerry's private, personal instrument of devilish torture, agreed to come over after we told him that there might be a Satanic presence in my parents' home.

Pro later told me that some of our guests were convinced to make an appearance after Pro gave them a choice. He told them, "We'd like you there breathing and alive. However, I could arrange for you to attend as a dead person. It's up to you."

Uncle Guido made sure that Barnardo Scrotari was there. He was Maria's brother, the one who wanted to cut another breathing passage in my throat when Uncle Guido, Pro and I visited the Scrotari headquarters and dance hall.

My Uncle Guido and Pro even convinced Desalvo Scrotari, the titular head of the entire despicable Scrotari clan, to attend. By the way, I have no idea what "titular" means, unless it refers to the fact that Desalvo was fat enough to have tits.

On the big night, I was waiting at my parents' doorway when our guests to arrive. I was polite and charming to every one of them.

Over and over again I said, "So pleased that you could make it," "Charmed to have you in our humble abode," "You look prettier (or more handsome) than the last time we met," or "Have you lost weight? You look especially marvelous tonight."

I hoped to lull the murderer into a false sense of confidence. It was working pretty well until Freedom Plenty complimented me on my fine Ricardo Montalban impression. She might have been the only one to see through my strategy. There was no harm in that because she wasn't a suspect.

I handed out name tags for everyone and they listed the person's name above a title which said, "Murder Suspect." One exception was Freedom Plenty, who didn't need a name tag because everyone in the known universe knew her. She insisted in being like everyone else, so I quickly created a name tag for her. It said, "Freedom Plenty / Famous, Nice Person."

I even suggested that in fairness Uncle Guido and Pro should wear name tags because, well, their professions would indicate that they might actually be suspects. But they would have no part of that idea. Pro said, "Look, I don't care if you are the boss's nephew, try to put that on me and I'll pin it to your prick and light it like a cigar."

It was a rather graphic suggestion, and it led me to embrace the idea that Uncle Guido and Pro would not wear name tags because it seemed a shame to upset the only relatives who would be there to witness my moment of triumph. Also, I wanted to be alive for the reading of Uncle Guido's will rather than the other way around. Since I didn't have a will, Uncle Guido would have to wait a good long time for the reading and that might upset him even further.

Martha arrived carrying her famous jubilee surprise, a red and green Jell-O mold with fresh bananas floating between the layers.

I said, "Oh, Martha, you shouldn't."

"It's a little nothing," Martha insisted, "I do it to help out any party Morty and I are invited to."

"No, you shouldn't," I interrupted, "because this isn't a party. It's a murder investigation."

"I just thought it would be nice," she pouted. "Maybe you could save it for after?"

"After what?" I asked.

"After the investigation is over," she said. "By the way, do you know my husband, Morty?"

"Nice to meet you, sir," I smoothly lied. "You are lucky to have such a beautiful and spirited wife."

"Thank you," Morty said, but he sounded as if were choking with the words.

Barnardo and Desalvo Scrotari, the next to arrive, were constantly muttering under their breaths. I think they were saying a mantra of some sort and it went something like "the only good Testosteroni is a dead Testosteroni."

There was a difficult moment when I greeted them at the door and reached out to shake their hands. Uncle Guido stopped me and said, "That ain't necessary. Anyway, if you touch them, you're going to have to wash your hands."

Desalvo growled, "Kiss my ass, Testosteroni."

Then, Bernardo, Desalvo, Uncle Guido and Pro all began shouting "Hey, you kiss my ass."

Very quickly, it became a rising crescendo of orders to plant someone's lips on one's own nether parts. That was when it suddenly occurred to me that perhaps that phrase referred to some ancient greeting ceremony between rival factions. I thought how quaint it would be if the four of them actually began smooching each other's asses before I began my interrogation of the suspects.

How different this world would be if Israeli and Palestinian, Taliban follower and American troops, Irish Catholics and Protestants and so many others were forced to osculate each other's asses before continuing the battle or the argument. Perhaps this would result in more harmony as people learned to love kissing each other's asses.

Of course, it could become the opposite and engender so much disgust that the combatants would fight more ferociously. Any hopes of settling arguments or of world peace in our time might be dashed.

So once again, I decided to keep such ideas to myself until I could find the better time to reveal them.

I stepped into the middle of the shouting quartet and yelled, "OK, OK, enough's enough. If there's any ass kissing to be done around here, I'll do it."

I guess that idea was so amazing to them that all four men immediately shut up. They also seemed to be seeing me in a different light, although I'm not sure what that was.

Subsequent to the amazing events of that night, several people have asked me if I knew the identity of the killer or killers at that point. It was a question I was asking myself at the time and the answer was: no. I had no idea.

I was flying by the seat of my pants and utilizing the well-known scientific forensic theory that might be briefly summarized thusly: "Throw enough shit on the wall and some is bound to stick."

After all the suspects were gathered together, I gave my little introductory speech, which I had rehearsed several times by talking to a mirror in the bathroom. The talk was so effective in that setting that twice my reflection confessed to murder. Unfortunately, the admission was not to killing Jerry Andrews or Thurmond Howarth, so I let my reflection go with a warning.

I began, "What you are about to see may be shocking for some of you. It might even make you retch uncontrollably. On the other hand, it could be a turn on if you are the kinky sort of person who enjoys sex with dead people or with unhappily married Jewish women. But that is another story for another time."

While giving each of them my best accusatory stare, I said, "But for one of you, for the ultimately guilty party, it will be an overwhelming experience. You will not be able to speak or breathe. Then one, two, three, badda-bing, badda-bang, as a result of this shocking scene, we will solve the murders of two of Sears Point's finest citizens and you will be scheduled for a lethal injection or to sit on the electric toaster that never forgives."

No one applauded, but I could tell that they were impressed with my eloquence. As I led the suspects through the living room, I thought that perhaps I should have added something memorable as a conclusion. It might be a great quotation like, "Ask not what you can do for your country," "Ich bin eine Berliner," "An old soldier never dies" or "Four score and seven years ago"—something to add the gravity that the situation. But then I thought that announcing in German that I was a resident of Berlin probably might not have the desired effect and might even lead to snickers, which would have ruined the mood.

I led them into my bedroom, which was pitch black. The shades had been drawn, the curtains closed and my Mickey Mouse night light with the nose that always glowed a comforting red was turned off.

The group was very quiet, possibly because my talk had impressed them. Without any conversation, without even a shuffling of their feet, they stood around the bed, apparently waiting for what would happen next.

I whispered, "Is everyone here?"

Uncle Guido counted and said, "...9...10. That's it. All present and accounted for."

As I reached for the light switch, I warned, "In order for this to have the right effect, you must stare at the scene I am about to reveal. No one can close their eyes or cover them with their hands. Uncle Guido, Pro and I will make sure of that. Here we go, in three, in two, in one...lights and action!!"

And I switched on the light, which was suddenly quite bright in the darkened room.

There was an audible gasp from the assembled suspects, which was a good sign. What they were seeing would surely have an effect on them and hopefully would provide the jolt that would create a breakthrough in my investigation.

164

It took a while for my eyes to become accustomed to the light and for my brain to analyze just what I was seeing.

Eventually, I could see that Jerry was still stretched out on the bed, and the slightly blue tinge to his skin had mostly disappeared, although it was obvious from the hoar frost around his lips and eyelids that he was still very frozen.

Then I could just barely discern that someone was kneeling over Jerry's middle.

In another second or three, I understood that the someone appeared to be a beautiful woman clad only in a black thong panty.

The someone was not moving.

A low groaning could be heard coming from the odd duo in front of me. I knew it couldn't be coming from Jerry.

I stepped closer, but the person's long blonde hair obscured her face.

As if in a daze, I reached forward and pulled back the hair.

That's when our group of suspects released the oddest melange of sounds. There were some sighs and moans of pleasure, but there were also retching noises and other indications of deep disgust. The sounds melded together to form the distinctive aural signature of a fen sinking into gaseous decline.

Then I could see why the suspects had those reactions.

It was Amanda, the lust of my life, who was kneeling over Jerry Andrews.

Amanda, in whom I had invested so many of my best fantasies, was giving a blow job to the corpse.

I reeled backward in surprise and amazement.

Almost immediately, I felt a deep sense of betrayal. I have since consulted several prominent psycho-therapists and they have all said that was the proper emotion when confronted by the scene I was observing.

I thought, why him and not me? Why would she give that much pleasure to a dead man before I had the opportunity? Did a dead man beg as much or as well as I? Would a dead man move or moan as much as me? Would a dead man be as grateful as me? What was going on here?

Amanda was looking at me and tears were flowing down her cheeks. As a person, the suspects immediately said, "Awwww."

"Amanda," I pleaded, "What are you doing to that stiff's stiff?" Although that much was obvious, I wanted to give her a chance to explain.

She mumbled something like, "Grmph mph mph gggle," or words to that effect. Obviously her parents had failed to teach her not to speak with her mouth full.

Amanda began shaking her head back and forth and up and down while emitting a series of unintelligible squeaks and squeals.

"Oh, Amanda," I cried as my heart was breaking, "Don't get so involved with him in front of me. Have you no mercy? You're breaking my heart."

That was when Elmer, the plumber, asked, "Hey, is that corpse fresh frozen?"

"Not so fresh," Pro answered, "But frozen, yes."

Elmer observed, "May be she's stuck on the guy?"

"Oh, please, don't tell me that she loves that carcass," I wailed. "This is the worst day of my life. I'm going to lose my girl to the rancid romancing of some remains. Why would she slurp a corpse's canolli before mine?"

"I don't think Elmer means 'stuck,' as in 'involved'," my solicitous Uncle Guido told me. "He was referring to 'stuck' as some kid's tongue might be on a lamppost when it's 10

166

below zero and his buddies challenged him to lick it. Maybe Elmer knows something."

Frantically Amanda tried to shake her head up and down indicating agreement with Uncle Guido.

"If that's right," I ordered, "quick, somebody bring me some boiling water."

"Why?" Asked Uncle Guido.

"Two reasons," I said. "First, I always wanted to say that during an emergency. And second we need to defrost him."

Uncle Guido enthused, "Good idea. Let's all also get in bed with them. Our bodies could provide enough heat to do the trick."

I was going to say that it might get a little uncomfortable if I tried to pour boiling water on Mr. Andrews and the suspects got in the way, but I decided not to. Why say anything which might be criticism of my Uncle Guido?

All the suspects began joining the corpse although there was a little grumbling about being forced to go to bed with a dead man. I warned, "Everyone keep your hands off Amanda. She's mine."

Amanda's muffled moans, which could have been protests of love for me or merely protests, eventually subsided as the suspects piled themselves on the bed—and on Amanda--like cord wood.

I resisted the urge to shout, "monkey pile," a childhood activity, that involved leaping on and squashing my friends.

I left the room to put some water in a pot and start it boiling. Quickly realizing the scientific principle that a watched pot never boils, I returned to the bedroom where I was overjoyed to hear Amanda's sweet voice coming from the bottom of the monkey pile. She was saying with her typical angelic gentleness, "Get the fuck off me, you bunch of turds," although her articulation left something to be desired because she sounded like she was speaking with a Dove Bar in her mouth.

When everyone untangled, we returned to our original positions with the suspects gathered in a rough circle around my bed. We were all staring at the stiff's as-yet erect member and a magnificently topless Amanda sitting next to the corpse.

The other people in the room were speechless. However, because of my training as a detective and man about town, I was able to ask, "Amanda, why the hell were you...?"

I had a disgusted look on my face and I waved a dismissive gesture in the direction of the corpse.

But before I could finish my question, Amanda began sputtering, "I took pity on you. You and your hopeless, endless begging for sex. Your constant whining, your annoying pleading. So I thought I was a little abrupt in firing you. You had worked hard on the Chad case and I thought you deserved a special reward, a little surprise tip just from me. I snuck into your room in the dark and damn. Damn and double damn!! One lick and I was stuck to that ice statue. Why would anyone in his or her right mind put a sculpture of an iceman in his bed?

"Amanda," I said as gently and as lovingly as I could, "That was no statue. That was a frozen corpse."

Well, I probably could have predicted that news wouldn't make Amanda feel any better. It took a long, silent beat before Amanda fully understood what I had revealed to her.

Then she shouted, "Gaaaack," and ran from my bedroom. We could hear her gagging well before she reached the bathroom.

Being an understanding guy who understood the soul of a woman, I followed her into the toilet and whispered in her ear as she knelt before the porcelain throne, "Don't let a little thing like this discourage you. You know that once you've been thrown from a horse, the best thing to do is to get right back in the saddle again."

I was pretty sure that would help Amanda psychologically get over this trauma and I hoped that it would also position me at the go-to guy should she ever decide to do it again. She looked up at me with the nicest, most loving expression (although she later told me at that moment she wanted to stab me many times with an ice pick).

But I was not about to allow Amanda's unfortunate incident to sidetrack my quest to find the murderer. Now that I could turn my full attention the gathering of suspects, I proceeded to next stage as planned.

"Follow me," I ordered and led all the suspects down the hall to the adjoining bedroom.

Desalvo Scrotari became confused during the 20-foot walk and began turning in circles, preventing the others from getting past him. That gave Uncle Guido and Pro a chance to get ahead of the suspects.

The human traffic jam was unsnarled when I went to Desalvo, told him to stand still for a moment or two and then turned him in the right direction. I wondered how Desalvo Scrotari could plan the murders of two people and function as the titular head of the Scrotaris when he couldn't walk down a short hallway and find the spare bedroom in my parents' home.

However, Desalvo remained a suspect because my motto has always been: once a suspect, always a suspect. That has saved me lots of time even when I am not investigating a baffling series of murders. For instance, with that in mind, I never have to smell a milk carton or a tub of old cottage cheese twice. I know for certain that once such things smell sour, they always will, and out they go.

Once all the suspects were crowded in the bedroom, I shouted to Uncle Guido and Pro, "Let your flashlights shine."

Two flashlights illuminated Thurmond Howarth's blue, frozen body still clad only in big, clunky construction boots.

Then, as we had planned, Uncle Guido and Pro quickly shined their flashlights on each of the faces of the suspects so I could note their reactions. It is well known that, when people look at a corpse, the true murderer will flinch and look away. Of course, almost anyone who looks at a corpse will flinch and look away, but murderers are supposed to do this in a particularly guilty manner.

However none of the suspects did anything out of the ordinary. Not a single suspect fell to his or her knees and confessed, as I hoped they would. At that moment, for the first time, it occurred to me that, if they were brave enough to strangle two nearly nude men, they might be up to the task of looking directly in their victim's distorted faces.

After Uncle Guido, Pro and I stared at each face of the suspects, there was a momentary, hushed pause. Then George Svaboda said, "Nice boots," putting him on the top of my list of suspects. He was the only person to praise the footwear of either corpse. But if he killed Thurmond because he admired his boots, why didn't George take them with him? The mysteries were getting more and more confusing the longer I thought about them.

Unfortunately, despite taking them to another room to view a completely different dead body, it was difficult to get the suspects' minds off the previous sight of a beautiful, topless woman in a thong panty giving a blow job to a frozen corpse. Jim Gerlund asked the question on many minds, "Why was Jerry's body treated so royally by your girlfriend while Thurmond was ignored?"

Since there was no answer to the question, I asked everyone to return to the bedroom with Jerry's body. There were some complaints about being forced to walk back and forth in a narrow hallway, but everyone went along with my request. This time Desalvo was able to find my bedroom with no difficulty at all.

In the old days in Chicago, the police would take a suspect from station to station, confusing him and eventually getting a confession from him. (I always thought that such confessions should begin with "Being only barely of sound mind and body...") I hoped that walking back and forth between bedrooms would accomplish the same thing, but unfortunately it did not. All the suspects knew exactly where they were and none were disposed to confess when we once again gathered around Jerry Andrews' remains.

Without allowing any of the tension to dissipate, I turned my attention to the quiet but insistent grass cutter George Svaboda. Knowing the importance of a forceful first question, I asked, "So George, how long have you thought of yourself as a shoe critic?"

George shrugged as if he didn't fully understand the question. I knew that pretending not to know all sorts of stuff was a typical ploy of a guilty person.

I proceeded to stare at him in an accusatory manner for a long time until George asked me, "Do you have an upset tummy, Tony?"

"No," I howled.

"You look peckish. Do you need a Tums?" George asked.

"Indeed not," I responded. "I need you to concentrate."

"I am," he said, "but I can't get what that woman was doing out of my mind. Do Americans often do that to corpses? Is it an added funeral expense?"

"George, we need to concentrate on the murders," I insisted. I also frowned to indicate how exasperated I was.

I decided to get right to the point with him mainly because I feared his attention span was limited. I demanded, "Am I not correct in saying that you were angry not because Jerry Andrews accused you of poisoning plants, but because Jerry told all the neighbors that you had a small penis. Am I right? And did this not drive you to thoughts of revenge? You wanted to cut off his head with hedge clippers, didn't you? Didn't you?"

As George repeatedly shook his head indicating that he was denying my logical accusations, Uncle Guido tugged on my arm. He said, "Uh, Tony..."

"Please, Mon Uncle, not when I'm going for the gold in my race to find the murderer."

George asked, "When did he say that stuff about my penis?"

"A good detective never reveals how he came to his conclusions," I said, refusing to be sidetracked. "Now don't play the stupid potted plant with me. You were angry, you were so upset you thought about using a pruning shear on Jerry's private parts so they would be as small as yours. And all because of a comment, a joking reference to your small pee pee. But smaller than your joint was your mind. You couldn't bear the fact that everyone in Sawmill was making fun of you behind your back, calling you pencil dick, the micro marauder, tiny tuba and so on. You..."

Uncle Guido insisted, "Uh, Tony...I think..."

Since my train of thought, which was just getting beyond the boxcars of accusation to the locomotive of intent, was quite derailed, I said, "Yes, well, Uncle Guido what could be so important that it requires you to interrupt my effort to get a confession from our smallest member over here?"

Uncle Guido then whispered to me, "It was small peonies. Small flowers. Jerry accused George of growing small peonies because he claimed that George didn't use the right fertilizer. It had nothing to do with his, you know." Uncle Guido was pointing at his own crotch.

"OK, I understand," I said. "Flowers? Are you sure it was about flowers?"

"Yes." Uncle Guido seemed very certain.

Standing tall in a dignified manner, I said to George, "Oh, well, never mind. But don't leave the room. You may be a suspect for some other crime before I'm done."

172

"There was no way Jerry would ever see my purple-veined love muscle because I always keep it tucked in my pants where it belongs." George was near tears.

"Just forget what I said," I advised him. Then raising my voice, I demanded, "I want everyone in this room to erase from their minds anything they heard about George having a sub-par schwantz. For all we know it might be huge, a work of monstrous art. There, George, does that make you feel better?"

But George, who was shaking his head, mumbled, "One year I had the biggest peonies in the state. They were called the peonies with personality, but no one can do that every year."

Since there was no reasoning with the man, I turned to the next suspect: Merry Martha. But before I could ask my first question, Martha said, "Look, sport, did you ever want to make it with a dead person the way that woman did?"

"Well, no, not really," I admitted, "Although occasionally my dates have fallen asleep during my 'corpus delickato.' It happened twice, no three times, with three different women. It didn't interfere with my pleasure and apparently they needed their sleep."

I said to her, "Martha McConklin, you had motive and opportunity to kill both Jerry and Thurmond. You had affairs with both men and both dumped you because they were experiencing difficulties walking after their sessions with you, am I not right?"

She proudly said, "You seemed to walk all right after visiting me all those times when my husband was working in the city."

All the suspects said in unison, "The cad." Well, some said "The crud," and others "The Kurd," obviously incorrectly believing that I was related to rebels in Iran.

Then I noticed Martha's husband Morty, who was looking a lot like one of his wife's jubilee surprise Jell-O molds. His face was turning red and green and something

173

that looked like chewed bananas was coming out of his nose.

Trying to get the discussion back to the two defrosting bodies, I directly accused Martha, "Can you prove that you did not kill both these men?"

"Don't you know you cannot prove a negative?" Martha sneered. "For instance, can absolutely prove that you have never made love to a chicken?"

"Although I am asking the questions here—not you—I am able to assure you that never happened, except possibly after the homecoming football game in my senior year in high school," I said. "I can't remember anything that happened after 8:30 that night and besides the chicken was old enough to know better."

"I take it all back," Martha said. "You are not a pinhead. You are a feather-brained idiot."

Hoping to forestall a jealous reaction from Morty, I walked up to him and asked, "No hard feelings?"

"None," Mort guaranteed, "As soon as you're dead."

I couldn't run off to South America in the midst of my summation to the suspects, so I continued by calling on Sheriff Clem, who immediately said, "I've been thinking real hard and, as far as I know, what we saw here with that young woman pleasuring a frozen corpse is not against the law mainly because no one I know had ever thought of doing that. But I will tell you this much, if I have anything to say about it, the city council will make that sort of behavior illegal in these parts. It seems like a horrible imposition on the corpse."

Wanting to get his mind off Amanda and the human Popsicle, I quickly asked, "Sheriff Clem, is it true that you took bow and arrow target practice on the night before both murders?"

174

"Tony Testa, I fire at least two quivers of arrows every night of the week," Sheriff Clem said. "So it's not unusual that I was at the range on the night before the murders."

I asked, "And isn't it true that you hated both Jerry and Thurmond because they seduced your daughter Melanie?"

"Let's just admit that my daughter is a very generous person," Sheriff Clem said. "She has probably shacked up with every man in this Burgoyne, Cherokee and Grant counties. That long list would include you Tony, as I recall. If I got angry at every man who ever touched her, I'd be the biggest mass murderer the world has ever known."

"I thank you for your candor, sheriff," I said. "And, by the way, I only got to second base with your daughter although I thought I had a good possibility of stealing third."

"Elmer, as our plumber," I began, but Omittus quickly interrupted and said, "If I ever decided to kill anyone—and I never have--my preferred method would be drowning, so count me out as a suspect."

"Not quite so fast," I said. "I reserve the right to question you later this evening if it turns out that I have overlooked something important, such as the fact that you murdered your mother and buried her under the concrete of the cellar of your house where her moans are heard to this day."

"Fat chance of that ever happening," Elmer sneered.

Now I just hate it when people sneer at me (don't you?), so I warned him, "Watch yourself, Elmer. Anything you say now or then or forever more can be held against you provided you hold nothing, especially your sweaty stinking body, against me. Furthermore, I may hold anything I want against you, including but not limited to cookware, bottles of Crisco (especially if you use that product to anoint yourself as former Senator and former Attorney General John Ashcroft is reported to have done), a Smithfield ham or a French tickler, if such items are needed as part of my investigation. Do you understand your rights?"

Elmer grouched, "I understand that I'm fucked."

Satisfied that I had put Elmer on notice, I turned my attention to Father Damian. The good priest immediately requested, "I would love to hear that Amanda's confession. Would you mind suggesting to her that I am a very modern priest in every way?"

After indicating that I would, I revealed, "Father, you seemed to admire Jerry's member as much or more than anyone else..."

"Yes," Father Damian said. "I wanted him to return to the confessional so I could anoint him with fine holy oils. That might have solved his problem. It certainly would have been a spiritual moment for me."

"So you're saying you wanted to save him," I concluded. "Therefore, murder would have been..."

The priest completed my thought, "Beside the point."

Once I understood what he was saying, I asked, "Are you in the habit of telling the truth?"

"Tony, I'm a priest," Father Damian said. "Doesn't that imply that I have some moral sensibilities?"

It did, but that didn't leave the Father off the hook. I promised myself to look up Catholic Church law to find out if a priest can ask for a momentary time out from being religious. Who knows, those guys might simply be able to do what we did in the playground when we were younger. Back then, our rules indicated that if we crossed our fingers behind our backs while we were speaking, we didn't have to tell the truth. Could that possibly apply to priests as well? Maybe a lot of what they say is spoken while they cross their fingers behind their backs.

(Incidentally, ever since elementary school, I have assumed that a lot of what is said by politicians, Presidents, CEOs and TV weather forecasters is spoken while their fingers are crossed behind their backs. That assumption makes it a lot easier to understand what such people are saying and I advise you to try believing it the next time you hear one of them speak.)

Nonetheless, I turned my attention to the next suspects. "Barnardo and Desalvo Scrotari," I said. "You have always plotted the downfall of my family."

"Yah, but wait a minute," Barnardo said. "You stopped things too soon with that Amanda broad. We had a bet on whether she could get the corpse off. If she can bring a corpse around, we could make her a fortune in Las Vegas or anywhere in the world. Here take my card. Get her to sign with us and we'll give you 10 per cent of whatever she earns."

"I'd need 15 per cent," I demanded, "Even though I am appalled that you would ask that kind of favor from me."

"12.5 and it's a deal," Barnardo said. "If she can bring the dead to life, that percentage could make you a billionaire."

"Thank you for giving me this opportunity to help mankind," I said, turning to Jim and Dottie Gerlund. "Didn't Thurmond say that your century plant was a fake and made out of paper? And didn't Jerry leave his socks in your bedroom after he was done porking your wife?"

"Both are true," Jim said, "But neither is sufficient reason to kill two men unless you believe I am a madman."

"Ah, the cuckoo defense," I surmised, "perhaps we should leave that up to a jury of your peers?"

Jim responded, "A jury of century plant growers? Kind of tough to find."

"Don't press me," I warned. At that point, I had accused all the suspects and none of them admitted to the murders. All remained suspects, but no person stood out from the group as the obvious perpetrator.

This was a difficult moment, known technically (and I apologize in advance for including phrases in this manuscript which could best be interpreted by seasoned professionals), in the detecting game as being, "Up shit's creek without a paddle."

"All right, we can see that each of you in this room had the motives and opportunity. Now, by the powers vested in me..."

George Svaboda asked, "What powers?"

"Because I'm a detective, I notice and understand things that ordinary people would miss," I said.

Jim Gerlund observed, "Sort of like after I've dusted and my wife sees a lot of motes that I missed?"

Refusing to stoop to the level of analogies about cleaning, I raised myself to my full height and again looking accusingly at everyone in the room. I said, "I have outlined all your motives and you have responded, as I guessed you would, with reasons for your innocence."

(Actually, with no one stepping forward to confess, making my job a lot easier, I would be forced to figure out which one of them did it. Once I made that deduction, then I would have to go to line 27 and enter the total gross income minus the appreciated self interest employment tax as per schedule...)

Note to self: do not think of your tax return while accusing a large group of people of murder. It's distracting.

"Actually, the easiest solution would be to say that you all did it," I stated with great confidence. "Agatha Christie did exactly that in her book 'Murder In The Calais Coach'—sorry if I ruined that novel for you with that revelation. I always thought it was kind of cheap to say that every Tom, Dick and Harry in the coach was the murderer."

I took this opportunity to offer a little education to the assembled suspects. I said, "And what about her silly detective, Hercule Poirot? I happen to know what Poirot means in French. A leak is a poireaux. And a wart is a poireau. What kind of a name is Hercule Wart? For that matter, who would name their little innocent kid of Hercule? It sounds like someone trying to clear a bit of macadamia nut from the back of their throat. His parents must have hated him. And another thing..."

178

Uncle Guido then reminded me, "None of us in this room are getting any younger. A few of the people here look like they just ate their afternoon dish of prunes before coming over here. They might need to visit the washroom facility in a hurry if you don't move these proceedings along."

"Sure, sure," I agreed, increasing the pace of my summation. "The other method of solving a murder is for me to suddenly announce that someone none of us ever heard of is the killer, thus proving I'm brilliant and you're not. But I will do better: I actually intend to solve these crimes."

I paused. When no one applauded, I continued, "Uncle Guido, when you looked at Jerry's arms, how were they placed?"

"Straight up, over his head, just the way you and I found him."

"Thank you, Uncle Guido," I said triumphantly. "Now I want everyone to think about Jerry's arms and ask themselves 'Is this a message from the grave?' Was Jerry trying to tell us something? Or was the killer communicating some deeply felt inner need?"

Elmer Omittus quietly said, "Looks like a referee saying the guy scored a touchdown."

"Very good," I said, with just a hint of the condescension he deserved. "Could his arms be in the shape of a letter? If it is a letter, what letter? And, I submit, could the letter be a 'Y'?"

"A 'Y'?" asked Father Damian. "Why a 'Y'?"

"Yes, father, I would expect you to ask the existential questions," I responded. "Indeed, why a 'Y'? Before answering that question, Sheriff Clem, will you go into the next bedroom, look at Thurmond Howarth's body and tell me what you observe about the position of his arms."

When he got there, Sheriff Clem shouted back at us from my parents' bedroom, "They're both touching the top of his head, kind of like he's a sergeant telling his platoon to form up on him. Or maybe he was just checking to make sure his toupee was on straight."

"Very good, except I submit that Thurmond Howarth did not wear a toupee," I said. "Check out that fact, Sheriff, if you will. Attempt to pull the hair off his scalp."

The suspects were reacting to my order by saying things like, "Yuk," "Do you have to?" and "May I be excused?"

Sheriff Clem shouted from the bedroom, "The hair is all his."

"You can come back now," I said. "I submit that the placement of the arms are the result of neither military signals nor vanity, but they form the letter 'M.'"

Father Damian said, "A 'Y' and an 'M'? I don't see what..."

"Neither did I until I asked myself: what does 'Y' and 'M' spell?" I was brilliant, if I do say so myself, even though I still wasn't sure at that point what anything meant.

Desalvo Scrotari offered, "Those letters are in the word ' 'anymore.' Maybe they're saying 'anymore of this will give me a headache.'"

Pro slapped him in the back of the head and said, "I'll give you a headache you'll never forget. Now shut up and let the kid talk."

I continued, "Actually that was pretty clever, but 'Y' and 'M' are also half of the letters 'YMCA,' and that is a song made popular by a group called the Village People."

George interjected, "I don't see what that has to do with the price of potatoes."

But it did. Well, actually it had nothing to do with the price of spuds, but I took that as a metaphor George was offering, even if he couldn't possibly know the definition of a metaphor.

180

At this point I very patiently explained that the Village People, "Were a singing group that attempted to represent Americans by dressing as a cop, a cowboy, a construction worker, a military man, a hippie and... an Indian!"

"That's my nephew," Uncle Guido said proudly. "He just answered why those stiffs were wearing moccasins and construction boots."

Elmer asked, "Was Jerry Andrews a member of the Village People? He never told me that and I don't think it was something he would have hidden from us. If he was a member of any group that actually made records, Jerry would be singing that from the highest rooftops in Sears Point."

"Which are not all that high seeing as Sears Point has only single family dwellings with a main floor and an attic at most," I pointed out. "Be that as it may, Jerry Andrews was not a member of the original Village People. He belonged to a new group who wanted to perform the Village People hits like 'Macho Man,' 'In the Navy' and 'YMCA.' Jim Gerlund, perhaps you can tell us why this new version of the Village People was going to perform in the nude?"

After looking shocked, after hesitating and beginning to sweat, Gerlund admitted, "We were going to be Saw Mill's answer to 'The Full Monty.' It was for a good cause--Viagra relief. There's a lot of men our age for whom Viagra is too expensive, such as the homeless. Do you know they don't allow people in mental institutions to have Viagra? We were going to raise money so any man or woman over age 65 who wanted Viagra could get it."

There was a round of polite applause from the other suspects. Encouraged, Jim Gerlund began shouting, "Then we'd get a constitutional amendment. We have a right to Viagra. Give me life, liberty and the pursuits made successful with Viagra."

"Please take it easy, Mr. Gerlund," I said. Then I probed, "And you rehearsed in my parents' cottage because it was usually empty. So tell us about Jerry Andrews and the Indian character?"

Jim very reluctantly said, "All his life that was the only part he wanted. Then he learned that two record producers saw someone named Felipe dancing in an Indian costume in Greenwich Village in 1976. The Indian was the first one in the group and there was never an opportunity to become the Native American for the Village People. Jerry hid his heart break until we began rehearsing. Then he begged and pleaded to be the Indian."

"But someone else wanted to be the Indian, didn't they? Am I right?" I probed.

"Me, because it's the best part," Jim Gerlund admitted. "You get to wear the headdress and run around in a loin cloth."

"But Jerry showed up in costume and did a hell of a rain dance, didn't he? Am I right?" I was being ruthless.

"Yes, yes," Jim cried, "But I didn't kill him."

"For now, I'm fairly sure you didn't," I assured him. "Let's turn to Thurmond, who always had a strange and annoying sense of humor. I'll bet he enjoyed kidding about Village People songs, especially 'In the Navy,' which for a time was accepted as a Navy recruiting song until someone told the Navy that the song wasn't what it seemed. Tell us about that, Jim?"

He sighed and began, "None of us ever believed the rumors about the Village People being gay and all. It never made any sense. After all, they sang 'Macho Man,' and what's more manly than that? But Thurmond wouldn't stop. He saw some sort of homosexual plot in 'YMCA' especially when we sang about the YMCA having everything for young men to enjoy. Even though it was impossible to convince him otherwise, we didn't believe him, not for a moment."

He paused before continuing, "When he began making fun of 'In the Navy,' well, that was just too much. Here was a patriotic song, but Thurmond continually pointed out that the

182

chorus had us chanting 'They want you, they want you.' We were about to vote him out of the group when he was murdered."

"And again, you expect us to believe that you did not kill him? Am I right? Am I right?" I was feeling confident at that point.

Jim said, "You am right. I am not a murderer."

"And again I believe you," I said.

Uncle Guido cautioned, "Aren't you being a little hasty? I mean, this guy had motive and opportunity both times, right?"

"Right," I agreed, "Jim felt threatened by Jerry's performance as an Indian and he was angry at Thurmond's irreverence about a group Jim loved, but he killed neither man."

Sheriff Clem shouted, "So who did? Do you think we've got all night? A rich handsome funny bachelor is going to propose tonight, and I want to see him get turned down. Big time."

"Everyone can understand that," I agreed. "So I'll get to the point. Dottie, was it difficult living with Jim and his Village People project?"

"Almost impossible," she said quickly. "He was so involved that he wanted to sell the house so I could live in a wigwam with him. And a lot of things he wanted me to do were beyond my talents. I was never any good at making the beaded belts he wanted me to sell, chewing pemmican was hell on my teeth and I never could pronounce 'kimo-sabe' correctly."

"Our hearts go out to you," I commiserated. "However, you must have known something was wrong. You were the one who sewed Jim's loin cloth."

Dottie sniffed, "It wasn't a big job." Her expression made it clear what she meant.

"Ever the dutiful wife," I said. "Even though you knew that this project was driving your husband crazy, especially when they decided to perform in the nude, making your loincloth unnecessary, you still loved him."

"Still do." She smiled and patted his forearm.

"And would do anything for him?"

When Jim tried to move towards me in a threatening manner, Uncle Guido stood behind him and said, "Don't even think about it."

"And isn't it true," I continued, "That you, Dottie Gerlund, were the Chicago park district archery champion in 1955, 1956 and 1958 under the name of Dorothy Chandler Grapenstein? Am I right? Am I right? That you might have gone to the Olympics in 1960 if you hadn't married Jim. Am I right? Am I right? "

Barnardo Scrotari told Pro, "One more 'am I right?' and I may stick an arrow in him myself."

"You don't think about it, neither," Pro warned.

Uncle Guido added, "Be grateful. At least he's not saying 'I submit' anymore."

Now I was ready to announce the identity of the murderer. I had fired accusations at nearly everyone in the room. I had all the suspects off balance and now I could go in for the crop de grass, a French phrase that loosely means "beating the lawn with the whip of truth."

"Dottie Gerlund," I said, as I pointed my right forefinger at her in a way that guaranteed that everyone would know who I was talking about. "I accuse you of the murder of Jerry Andrews because you wanted to protect your husband's part in the new Village People's performance during the Viagra Relief Show. Dottie Gerlund, I accuse you of the murder of Thurmond Howarth because your were afraid that, if your husband got any angrier at him, Jim would burst a blood vessel. I think you can take her away now, Sheriff."

That was when Dottie bit my finger. She munched hard on it and that hurt. I yelled, "Shit," and pulled it out of her mouth, scraping my knuckle on her teeth.

"Do you know how filthy the human mouth is?" I asked. "Even a dog's mouth is cleaner than yours and everyone knows that a dog uses his mouth to lick his balls."

I thought I had re-established control after Dottie's attack on me and I was about to repeat my request to the Sheriff to throw her in jail, when we all heard Jim Gerlund say, "Not so fast, me hearties."

(In fairness, I'm not too sure about the "me hearties" part because that sounds very nautical for old Jim. It is included here to heighten the dramatic impact.)

While all our eyes were on Dottie, Jim had somehow found the bow. Now he was pointing an arrow right between my eyes as he said, "After what she did for me today and over the years, the least I can do is play a little William Tell with you. Oh, my, you don't have an apple on your head, so I'll just have to put this arrow into your forehead without benefit of a Jonathan, Fuji, or a McIntosh."

"I wouldn't do that." I spoke very quietly yet with great determination even though I felt like screaming or begging.

"Why not?"

"It would give me the worst headache," I realized.

"Always with the jokes," Jim said. "We'll put a stop to that." And he drew back more on the bow string.

"This is something I never revealed to anybody," I said, speaking quickly. "All of Sears Point was built on an ancient Indian burial ground. Digging the foundations for your homes disturbed their spirits. Now all the skeletons, with skin hanging from their arm bones, are rising up to take this sacred ground back. It's just like in the movie 'Poltergeist.' All the skeletons are behind you right now. Don't look back or they'll jump you and take you into the grave with them. Don't look back, I implore you."

"Good try, shamus," Jim said. "I almost believed you."

Darn it. And I was just congratulating myself on coming up with a pretty snappy and believable story to distract him. It was my best shot, I took it, he didn't fall for it, and now what was I going to do?

My hands were up. The bow was beginning to quiver as if Jim couldn't maintain the tension of the string too much longer. Neither Uncle Guido nor Pro could get to me before an arrow shish-ka-bobbed me.

I was about to go down for the third time. I knew I was near death because a life began flashing before my eyes.

Unfortunately, it was not my life. For some odd reason, I began to see the life of Carol Tennyson, a girl I'd had a crush on from sixth grade until we entered high school. I saw her birthday parties and enjoyed the memory of the day she got a puppy as a pet.

As I experienced her life, I felt the shock of her first period and the pleasure of her first kiss. Just as things were getting good and I had hopes of seeing the first time Carol got laid, my brain tuned out of her life and returned me to my own, even though I found Carol's to be much more interesting than mine.

And I was still faced with an angry, frightened, protective husband and Village People wannabe who was about to skewer me with an arrow fired from six feet away.

There was only one thing to do. I began singing and waving my arms.

I sang, "Y." And both hands raised above my head to form the letter.

Then I shouted, "M." Both hands were on my head.

"C." Both arms to my right while offering a quick silent prayer that I did not join Jerry and Thurmond and add my letter "C" to their dead "Y" and "M."

"A." My arms formed a triangle over my head.

186

Then I shouted, "Everybody. Come on. I can't hear you." And I began to sing again.

All the suspects, and even Amanda, began singing "Y. M. C. A." It was a mad scene in that bedroom where only the corpse remained, well, stiff.

And I have to admit there was something irresistible about it. There we were, all Americans, singing our hearts out in unison, doing what we might not have done before Sept. 11, 2001 when we were all more divided. There was a feeling of intense patriotism to sing about a joyous place that has everything young men can enjoy. We could all agree— even the women—that the YMCA was a fun place to stay. And we could all imagine how much fun it would be to hang out there with all the boys.

I know that references to the horrors of Sept. 11 and to the patriotism that followed the crashes into the Pentagon and the World Trade Center may seem like cheap attempts to get the readers on my side. But I am serious: getting everyone in that room to join in singing "Y. M. C. A." was an achievement of which I am proud. You can laugh. You can place yourself among the scorned scoffers. But all the suspects, myself and even America were the better for it.

Finally, with the third run through of "Y. M. C. A.," Jim's arms began quivering. He could not help himself.

He tried to remain in his bow-threatening position, but the music and the group sing-along of his favorite song by his beloved group was beginning to get to him.

Dottie warned, "Jim, no, don't," but it was too late. When we all sang the third "A" of Y. M. C. A., Jim raised his bow over his head to form the triangle indicating that letter.

That's when I dived at him, attempting to shove him to the ground.

Uncle Guido pushed into him from the other side, putting his shoulder into a perfect cross-body block that would have stopped an NFL running back in his tracks.

Because Jim was already on the floor, Pro piled on top, trying to grab the bow.

Pro was only a little late and Jim managed to fire his arrow into the ceiling.

As I was trying to hold on to his arms to make sure Jim wasn't able to get another arrow ready for firing, I shouted, "Monkey pile! Monkey pile!!"

Without thinking twice, the other suspects plus Freedom and Amanda jumped on top of Jim.

There was a lot of squirming and struggling, pushing and shoving.

Jerry's partially frozen dead body fell off the bed into the monkey pile and I could hear Merry Martha scream, "The dead guy's dick is in my ear. God damn it, get him off me."

I could even hear Morty mumble, "There's only one dick going in your ear, baby, if I have anything to say about it."

Merry Martha shouted, "If you're talking to me, Morty, I can't hear you. I've got a dick in my ear."

There were other complaints. Elmer was wheezing, "I can hardly breath."

George Svaboda thought someone was pinching his ass. We later determined his discomfort was caused by the end of Jim's bow, which was rammed into George's rear.

Father Damian was yelling about praying together, but I was never sure exactly what Father Damian was praying for.

There was a lot of shouting and groaning until we all heard the gunshot. Then things got very quiet very quickly.

In the silence, Dottie announced in her best, sweet grandmotherly tones, "Get away from my husband, or I'll shoot your asses off."

After several minutes spent unpealing ourselves, we were all standing once again in the bedroom. Only this time we were looking at a determined grandmother holding what looked to me like a Glockenstein Mitgonger Einfarter 9mm., a model I happen to know a lot about because I used it to shoot at the Glockenspiel in Munich. The authorities were not pleased that I added two hours to the clock chimes even though I explained that it was a better version of Daylight Savings Time.

"My, what a big gun you have, grandmother," I said, stalling while I tried to figure out what to do.

"The better with which to kill you all, my dearies," Dottie said. She immediately got my award for the suspect with the best grasp of grammar. Imagine, correctly inserting the word "which" in a sentence while threatening mass murder so she would not end her thought with the inappropriate "with". I know of no one else who would have the presence of mind to do that. Dottie, you may be a murdering fiend, but you sure know how to parse a sentence.

I pleaded, "How can you hope to get away with what will be the largest—and only--mass murder in the history of Saw Mill, Michigan?"

"And I always wanted to be in the record books," Dottie sneered. "You gave me the perfect fall guys. You, yourself, talked about the poltergeists in these parts. They did it, they're already dead, case closed. What do you think of that?"

"Where did you get the pistol?" I asked.

"From some people more interested in grabbing my husband Jimmy's jimmy than securing their weapons," Dottie said. Then she waved the pistol in the direction of the chagrinned Pro, who noticed that the place on his belt in the middle of his back where he would normally carry his pistol was now empty.

He offered Uncle Guido a sad "What can you do, you can't win them all" shrug and Uncle Guido patted him on the back. My Uncle Guido was always such a good boss!

I asked, "Why did you do it, Dottie?"

"Why else?" She asked. "For love."

"And you hired the guy who threatened me while I was walking?" I inquired.

"No," she said proudly, "That was a freebie. When I described you to my cousin Ralphie, he begged to tap dance on your head."

"And you did kill both Jerry and Thurmond?" I was going to get to the bottom of this mystery even if it killed me. Oops, I shouldn't have even thought that. Mmmmm, attempting to erase that from my mind. Mmmmm.

"Stop that damned humming," Dottie ordered. "Yes, and I would have killed you, too, if you hadn't jumped into the bushes so fast."

"So you were the arrow shooter when Uncle Guido and I came home that night?"

"Enough talking, already," she ordered. "I've got to kill you all, make our escape and get to a manicure appointment in a half hour."

I observed, "That is so cold blooded."

"No, it isn't," Dottie protested. "You obviously don't know how difficult it is to get an appointment to have your nails done around here. OK, so who wants to be first?"

Almost all the suspects said, "Not me," followed by, "Him, first," indicating me. It was not the kind of popularity I wanted.

"All right, if I have to die," I said with all the dignity I could muster, "I'll die after I speak my last words. All right?"

When Dottie agreed, I began a filibuster, reciting from the Bible and Kahlil Gibran, revealing what I had learned in my life so far, bequeathing my worldly possessions one by one to people I knew who were not there in the bedroom with me, making requests—and then amending them—for last meals, finalizing funeral arrangements, covering

190

disposition of the body and contributions of body parts to science and medicine, etc.

At the end of one hour of constant talking, I could see that Dottie was getting sleepy. Her eyes were drooping (if the truth be known, so were mine—my soliloquy was that boring) and she looked as if she desperately needed a nap.

For my part, I was emphasizing certain words to encourage her trance. I said, "I have learned that SLEEP is important, that SLEEP knits the raveled sleeve of care, that now I lay me down to take my SLEEP, SLEEP perchance to dream, SLEEP walking like lady Macbeth."

In a stage whisper I pleaded with the suspects, "Come on, help me out here. I'm running out of material."

They lined up and began to whisper in my ear, after which I would repeat their quotes to Dottie. Thanks to Sheriff Clem, I intoned, "We are such stuff as dreams are made on; our little life is rounded with a SLEEP."

Father Damian helped me with, "I lay me down in peace to SLEEP," while Elmer offered, "Oh SLEEP! It is a gentle thing, beloved from pole to pole."

Somehow George was able to remember a terrific quote from Tennyson, "What e'er thy griefs, in SLEEP they fade away, to SLEEP! To SLEEP! SLEEP, mournful heart, and let the past be past: SLEEP, happy soul, all life will SLEEP at last."

I gave him a "thumbs up" in gratitude for the helpful quote.

With my brilliant beginning and with the help that the suspects provided, my "last words" seemed to be having the desired affect. When her eyes began to blink and close for longer periods of time, when Jim's head slumped down on his chest in a sympathetic nap-time, when the pistol she was holding began to droop, I leaped forward.

Unfortunately, I was a split second late and Pro grabbed the pistol away from her.

I quickly looked around. My last words had been too effective. Everyone in the room except Pro, Uncle Guido and I were hypnotized.

I later learned that the reason Pro did not fall under the hypnotic spell I was casting was because he was thinking about an upcoming hit on Lawrence "Wishbone" Manicotti. Instead of paying attention to what I was saying, he was considering the escape route, deciding on what to wear, and choosing the method of death.

Pro told me that the breakthrough for the problem came to him while I was talking. "Out of the blue, in a blinding flash, it occurred to me that we should take both his legs, pull in opposite directions and make a wish," Pro gleefully said. "It would save on the expense of ammunition, send a message not to mess with us and, who knows, maybe our wish would come true."

With his mind fully occupied on such thoughts, my sleep suggestions bounced off his cerebral cortex like a rubber bullet on a metal crotch protector.

Uncle Guido said he spent the time staring at Martha's breasts. "If they'd begin to talk, I, too, would have been hypnotized," he later revealed. "As it was, I was trying to figure out if they were real or surgically enhanced. Eventually I decided I didn't care, but that was the exact time when you made your move."

With Pro covering her with the pistol and with my tight grip on Dottie's arm, the situation was suddenly reversed: I had the advantage and I was younger and stronger than she was. Maybe, even handsomer.

I suddenly remembered something my Uncle Guido told me when I was still in knee pants in elementary school: never get into a fight that you can't win and never pick on an opponent who is bigger and stronger than you are unless you have a cannon.

There I was squaring off against a woman more than twice my age and half my weight. I was pretty sure this was fight I could win.

I cocked back my fist while holding Dottie at arm's length. I asked everyone in the room, "Should I? Should I?"

Then I remembered most of them were asleep. Any good detective always has a plan B and a plan C and even a D, so I shouted, "WAKE UP, YOU SLEEPY HEADS. TIME TO GET UP AND GET OUT OF YOUR HEAD." Then I snapped my fingers three times.

After most of the suspects were out of their trances, I asked them again, "Should I?"

Uncle Guido, who was never in a trance, advised me, "If you gotta ask, maybe you're not ready to do this."

"Nonsense," I announced.

Dottie pleaded, "I'm only a kindly little grandma."

Then Uncle Guido added, "Seems to me when someone's asking for it, they ought to be obliged."

I hauled back and popped her one right in the kiester. Then I shouted, "Dottie, you're giving grandmothers a bad name."

I know, I know. Some readers will be appalled that I punched a skinny crone in the snoot. Hopefully, others might applaud my application of rough, instant justice.

My attitude was, "She deserved it." What I didn't deserve was the infected knuckle I got after I punched her in the mouth. Dottie should have brushed her teeth a lot more often than she did.

I thought Dottie would go down like a sack of dried prunes, but I was wrong. She took the punch, but after her head snapped back, she was still standing and ready to brawl with me. All I could think of was: this grandmother could give Mike Tyson a run for his money.

I shouted, "Most good grandmas don't murder two men with a bow and arrow."

She replied, "Most good grandmas were never in the Marines."

Her right hand punched at my face and only quick reaction on my part enabled me to start to duck. I wasn't quite fast enough because she hit me with a glancing blow to my cheek bone, which immediately felt as if I received a shot of Novocain.

I had to think of something fast because there was no telling what an angry, protective, 110-pound former Marine and current AARP member overflowing with evil thoughts would do next.

So I kicked her. Right in the shins.

When she bent over to rub the spot where my lightning-fast punt got her in the uprights, I kicked her again in the other shin.

(For the uninitiated, the twin kicks to the shins were a maneuver I perfected as a 10-year-old in the playground. When defending yourself against any opponent who is smaller and weaker than you are, such as girls your own age before they went through puberty, shin kicking can be a very effective move.

(But do not try this at home and never practice on someone you love. A few seconds after the people you love stop howling in pain, almost anyone who has been shin kicked will come after their attacker with a blind fury. Speaking with the benefit of my own experience, anyone who said they loved you before you drop kicked their shins will find it very difficult to say afterwards. In fact, they are much more likely to say, "Get out of my life, you shit-head," or words to that effect.)

As I cocked my right fist preparing to deliver the knock out blow, Dottie punched at my balls. I was saved because the target was so small, but the blow hurt nonetheless.

Pro and Uncle Guido began laughing even though it was no laughing matter. I guess they thought my gasping and wheezing was funny. I did not.

Dottie closed in and began pounding my stomach with a furious tattoo of blows. Her fists were small, but when they landed in the right spot, they hurt.

I demanded of Pro, "Just shoot her, for damned sake."

Pro, who was laughing so hard he could barely breathe, said, "No honor in that. I'd be too embarrassed to go to prison for killing a grandma."

Uncle Guido sounded impatient when he said, "Tony, stop fooling around and just take care of business."

That was easy for him to say. His stomach wasn't becoming a senior citizen's punching bag. His balls weren't being rung like the chimes in Notre Dame Cathedral by an aging female Quasimodo bent on turning me into a castrato or a capon or a soprano.

I got angry. I got into a crouch, fending off Dottie's blows with my forearms. I waited until she began to tire herself out.

Then I stepped into my punch, delivering a perfect, straight, from-the-shoulder shot to Dottie's forehead.

She went down and no one had to count to ten. She was out.

I raised both arms and began dancing around in victory until Uncle Guido advised, "Cold cocking an old lady is hardly the Thrilla' in Manila. If I were you, I'd just skulk away in shame."

Chapter Ten

With Sheriff Clem right in the room, it wasn't necessary to call the police. I only had to make sure he was out of his trance and not confused. Once he understood what happened, he arrested Dottie and Jim, and charged them with the two murders.

Sheriff Clem later told me that, as long as he was at it, he also charged them with every other unsolved murder in Saw Mill and six adjacent counties. "That way we could clear the books of a lot of cases," the Sheriff said. "My deputies wanted to throw in Jimmy Hoffa, John F. Kennedy, Dr. Shepherd's wife, and a few others, but I told the boys to take it easy. We start putting those names on indictments and Geraldo Rivera or Jerry Springer might show up to get the story. Then this town would be in just a terrible mess."

Shortly after they were arrested, the Gerlund's lawyer immediately claimed that they were insane at the time of the murders. He claimed that because I tried to distract them by claiming that Native American skeletons, with skin hanging from their arm bones, were sneaking up on them, the Gerlunds were immediately driven round the bend by that image. If successful, this would be the first murder while under the influence of poltergeists defense.

A few days after my brilliant interrogation of the suspects, Freedom Plenty told me she had an interesting time witnessing the actual trapping and arrest of two murder suspects. She then disappointed me when she decided against interviewing me as the detective who once had two corpses in various freezers. She pursed her lips in a most fetching manner and said, "That might not be the most popular program I had ever done."

After I used a little gentle persuasion in the hopes of becoming a guest on her show (actually it was a lot of energetic begging and pleading), she added that any conversation with me might encourage others to put corpses in their freezers, which would adversely affect the funeral industry. Also she shuddered to think of the reaction of the studio audience if the conversation ever turned to women who give blow jobs to frozen corpses and the men who still loved them.

It has been almost two months since the Gerlunds' arrest. I am now working on the 72nd version of the Tony Testa Nationwide Detective Agencies Business Plan. The flow sheets I have developed demonstrate that, with a nationwide rollout creating 212 offices in virtually all cities in America, within 19 years and seven months we would achieve profitability. Of course, that depends on 20,000 wealthy women a day requesting the services of my Testa-dicks to find their straying husbands.

(The plan includes a $5 million a year consultant's fee to moi, which I would receive whether I actually contributed anything to the enterprise or not. I have been told that level of compensation is well within expectations.)

During the bullet-point presentations to venture capitalists, I use the Case of The Softening Critics and The Case of the Almost Nude Corpses in My Parents' Living Room as examples of my capabilities.

So far all the venture capitalists have said that they would "Consider the proposal," although none have committed actual funds. Every session with a V. C. includes at least one question about oral sex with a frozen corpse. I'm thinking of leaving that detail out of my future presentations.

Uncle Guido continues to tell me that he enjoys being a private detective and wants to work on more cases with me. He even suggested that he create a few crimes for me to "solve." While I thought it was a good idea and might actually create some good cash flow, the negatives it might bring on—from arrest to lethal injection—made it too risky for now. I did tell Uncle Guido that I appreciated his energy in pursuing new clients for us.

Solving the Jerry Andrews and Thurmond Howarth murders helped make my detective business better known in Sears Point and Saw Mill. While new cases haven't exactly been pouring in, I do well enough these days that I have moved up from eating beans and rice to eating beans and rice with chicken.

Most recently Merry Martha hired me because she thought she was the victim of a Peeping Tom. I didn't think it was necessary to get Uncle Guido involved in the case because it was so minor. That was why I staked out her house by myself.

Sure enough, about the time Merry Martha was getting ready for bed, a tall, skinny guy crept up to her window and looked at her as she undressed.

I surprised him when I quietly came up behind him and asked, "What do you think you are doing?"

He whispered, "Looking at that beautiful woman. Have you ever seen such breasts? And those legs!!"

Momentarily distracted from the assignment, I looked in Merry Martha's window and I had to admit that the Peeping Tom was right. She was just gorgeous. In fact, she seemed more attractive looking at her through a window than up-close and personal in her bed.

We both stared at her until she turned out the lights and went to bed. Then we shook hands and agreed to meet at the same place on Tuesday and Thursday nights, when I was free because my Amanda was attending her Group Therapy sessions.

I'm still not sure what, if anything, I should tell Martha about that arrangement. For now, I decided not to mention about my Tuesday-Thursday viewings with the Peeping Tom to Martha because it's a nice parallel to what happened when I started in the detective game. At the time, if you remember, I didn't tell Martha's husband, my client, that I was having an affair with her. That worked out pretty well for a long time. What I believe now is that what's good for the goose is good for taking a gander at the gander.

As for Amanda, she began to work with three different psychotherapists to get over the trauma of giving a blow job to a dead man. One of the guarantees about living in America in the 21st century is that, whatever you have done, no matter how strange or different, somewhere there is a group organized around that interest or fetish.

And that is probably why Amanda also found a group of people who have done awful (or, possibly from their point of view, romantic) things with corpses. Meeting on Tuesday and Thursday evenings, they called themselves the Daley Voters, after the 1960 presidential election when the dead of Chicago allegedly voted Jack Kennedy into office.

After her group encounters, Amanda usually calls me to talk about what she heard that night. In her group, there was a computer programmer who used grandpa as a Yule log, a schizophrenic woman who had mastered the art of ventriloquy so her husband could continue telling her children bedtime stories long after he died, and an accountant who enjoyed three-way sex with two corpses. After listening to the stories told in her group, Amanda usually feels a lot better about herself.

We see each other frequently and I am happy to report that everything is A-OK in the sex department, except for the fact that she begins choking if I kiss her for more than three seconds. She assures me that she might have done that in any case, so we both believe that she is doing a lot better.

Early next week Amanda should confront an important milestone testing her progress. That is when she will eat a Popsicle for the first time since the incident.

After that, she may very well turn her attentions to me and I'm hoping she won't then demand that the area of my body under closest consideration by me be as cold as a Popsicle. Only time will tell.

The End

Books from Science & Humanities Press

HOW TO TRAVEL — A Guidebook for Persons with a Disability – Fred Rosen (1997) ISBN 1-888725-05-2, 5½ X 8¼, 120 pp, $12.95 18

HOW TO TRAVEL in Canada — A Guidebook for A Visitor with a Disability – Fred Rosen (2000) ISBN 1-888725-26-5, 5½X8¼, 180 pp, $14.95

AVOIDING Attendants from HELL: A Practical Guide to Finding, Hiring & Keeping Personal Care Attendants 2nd Edn — June Price, (2002) paperback edition (2002) ISBN 1-888725-60-5, 8¼X6½, 200 pp, $18.95

The Bridge Never Crossed — A Survivor's Search for Meaning. Captain George A. Burk (1999) The inspiring story of George Burk, lone survivor of a military plane crash, who overcame extensive burn injuries to earn a presidential award and become a highly successful motivational speaker. ISBN 1-888725-16-8, 5½X8¼, 170 pp, illustrated. $16.95

Value Centered Leadership — A Survivor's Strategy for Personal and Professional Growth — Captain George A. Burk (2003) Principles of Leadership & Total Quality Management applied to all aspects of living. ISBN 1-888725-59-1, 5½X8¼, 120 pp, $16.95

Nursing Home – Ira Eaton, PhD, (2010) You will be moved and disturbed by this novel. ISBN 9781596300651, 5½X8½

300 pp, $16.95

Me and My Shadows — Shadow Puppet Fun for Kids of All Ages - Elizabeth Adams, Revised Edition by Dr. Bud Banis (2000) A thoroughly illustrated guide to the art of shadow puppet entertainment using tools that are always at hand wherever you go. A perfect gift for children and adults. ISBN 1-888725-44-3, 7X10, 68 pp, 12.95

MamaSquad! (2001) Hilarious novel by Clarence Wall about what happens when a group of women from a retirement home get tangled up in Army Special Forces. ISBN 1-888725-13-3 5½ X8½, 200 pp, $14.95

Virginia Mayo — The Best Years of My Life (2002) Autobiography of film star Virginia Mayo as told to LC Van Savage. From her early days in Vaudeville and the Muny in St Louis to the dozens of hit motion pictures, with dozens of photographs. ISBN 1-888725-53-27X10 270 pp, $16.95

The Job — Eric Whitfield (2001) A story of self-discovery in the context of the death of a grandfather.. A book to read and share in times of change and Grieving. ISBN 1-888725-68-0, 5½ X 8½, 100 pp, $14.95

Plague Legends: from the Miasmas of Hippocrates to the Microbes of Pasteur-Socrates Litsios D.Sc. (2001) Medical progress from early history through the 19th Century in understanding origins and spread of contagious disease. A thorough but readable and enlightening history of medicine. Illustrated, Bibliography, Index ISBN 1-888725-33-8, 6¼X8¼, 250pp, $24.95

Sexually Transmitted Diseases — Symptoms, Diagnosis, Treatment, Prevention-2nd Edition – NIAID Staff, Assembled and Edited by R.J.Banis, PhD, (2006) . Illustrated with more than 70 diagrams and photographs of lesions, ISBN 1-888725-58-3, 5½X8¼, , 298 pp, $18.95

The Stress Myth -Serge Doublet, PhD (2000) A thorough examination of the concept that 'stress' is the source of unexplained afflictions. Debunking mysticism, psychologist Serge Doublet reviews the history of other concepts such as 'demons', 'humors', 'hysteria' and 'neurasthenia' that had been placed in this role in the past, and provides an alternative approach for more success in coping with life's challenges. ISBN 1-888725-36-2, 5½X8¼, 280 pp, $24.95

Rhythm of the Sea —Shari Cohen (2001). Delightful collection of heartwarming stories of life relationships set in the context of oceans and lakes. Shari Cohen is a popular author of Womens' magazine articles and contributor to the Chicken Soup for the Soul series. ISBN 1-888725-55-9, 8X6.5 150 pp, $14.95

To Norma Jeane With Love, Jimmie -Jim Dougherty as told to LC Van Savage (2001) ISBN 1-888725-51-6 The sensitive and touching story of Jim Dougherty's teenage bride who later became Marilyn Monroe. Dozens of photographs. "The Marilyn Monroe book of the year!" As seen on TV. 5½X8¼, 200 pp, $16.95

Riverdale Chronicles—Charles F. Rechlin (2003). Life, living and character studies in the setting of the Riverdale Golf Club by Charles F. Rechlin 5½ X 8¼, 100 pp ISBN: 1-888725-84-2 $14.95

Bloodville — Don Bullis (2002) Fictional adaptation of the Budville, NM murders by New Mexico crime historian, Don Bullis. 5½ X 8½, 300 pp ISBN: 1-888725-75-3 $14.95

The Cut—John Evans (2003). Football, Mystery and Mayhem in a highschool setting by John Evans ISBN: 1-888725-82-6 5½ X 8¼, 100 pp $14.95

The Way It Was-- Nostalgic Tales of Hotrods and Romance Chuck Klein (2003) Series of hotrod stories by author of Circa 1957 in collaboration with noted illustrator Bill Lutz BeachHouse Books edition 5½ X 8¼, 200 pp ISBN: 1-888725-86-9 $14.95

"...a delightful mix of anecdote, observation, and social history. A book so masterfully written, you can almost smell new upholstery on the street rod. This is definitely the best read..."

Paul Taylor, Publisher. Route 66 Magazine

"...a classic recipe for hours of delightful entertainment.... If this is your first time reading Chuck Klein, it[1]s just like eating chocolate. Once you have the first bite, you know you[1]ll be coming back for more. "

The Way It Was

Nostalgic Tales of HotRods and Romance

Chuck Klein

Carl Cartisano, Cruisin[1] Style Magazine

a new American classic, conjuring up images of good, clean fun for the "hot-rodders" of yesterday and today....a fun, fast read that appeals to the kid in all of us." --

Aaron Lasky, Hot Rod DeLuxe, CK DeLuxe, & Kingpin Magazines

"Your book is great. You have captured the feel and texture of the 'fifties in each story. It's a wonderful read ...which accurately portrays and preserves the magic of the era".

Dusty Rhodes, WSAI Radio, Cincinnati

"As varied as the vehicles --a 1960 Corvette, a '57 Chevy, a 1937 Ford pick-up truck--and the people who drive them-- eager teenagers cruisin' for dates, a sailor on furlough, a young woman who understands a "two-eighty-three engine, bored sixty thousandths over"-- these well crafted tales are a veritable potpourri of American road lore." "Bet you can't read just one!"

Michael Lund, Author of the Growing Up on Route 66 Series

Route 66 books by Michael Lund

Growing Up on Route 66 — Michael Lund (2000) ISBN 1-888725-31-1 Novel evoking fond memories of what it was like to grow up alongside "America's Highway" in 20th Century Missouri. (Trade paperback) 5 X8, 260 pp, $14.95

Route 66 Kids — Michael Lund (2002) ISBN 1-888725-70-2 Sequel to *Growing Up on Route 66*, continuing memories of what it was like to grow up alongside "America's Highway" in 20th Century Missouri. (Trade paperback) 5 X8, 270 pp, $14.95

A Left-hander on Route 66--Michael Lund (2003) ISBN 1-888725-88-5. Twenty years after the fact, left-hander Hugh Noone appeals a wrongful conviction that detoured him from "America's Main Street" and put him in jail. But revealing the details of the past and effecting a resolution of his case mean a dramatic rearrangement of his world, including troubled relationships with three women: Linda Roy, Patty Simpson, and Karen Murphy. (Trade paperback) 5 X8, 270 pp, $14.95

Miss Route 66--Michael Lund (2004) ISBN: 1-888725-96-6. In this novel, Susan Bell tells the story of her candidacy in Fairfield, Missouri's annual beauty contest. Now married and with teenage children in St. Louis, she recounts her youthful adventure in this small town along "America's Highway." At the same time, she plans a return to Fairfield in order to right injustices she feels were done to some young contestants in the Miss Route 66 Pageant. Throughout this journey she wonders what, if anything, was feminine in the "Mother Road" of the 1950s. (Trade paperback) 5 X8, 270 pp, $14.95. .

AudioBook on CD-- Miss Route 66 ISBN: 1-888725-12-5 by Michael Lund unabridged 5 CD's --7 Hours running time. $24.95

Route 66 Spring-- Michael Lund (2004) ISBN: 1-888725-98-2. The lives of four young Missourians are changed when a bottle comes to the surface of one of the state's many natural springs. Inside is a letter written by a girl a dozen years after the end of the Civil War. Lucy Rivers Johns ' epistle contains a sad story of family failure and a powerful plea for help. This message from the last century crystallizes the individual frustrations of Janet Masters, Freddy Sills, Louis Clark, and Roberta Green, another group of Route 66 kids. Their response to the past charts a bold path into the future, a path inspired by the Mother Road itself. (Trade paperback) 5½ X8¼, 270 pp, $14.95.

Route 66 to Vietnam Michael Lund (2004) ISBN 1-59630-000-0 This novel takes characters from earlier works in the Route 66 Novel Series farther west than Los Angeles, official destination of the famous highway, Route 66. Mark Landon and Billy Rhodes find the values they grew up on challenged by America's role in Southeast Asia. But elements of their upbringing represented by the Mother Road also sustain them in ways they could never have anticipated. . (Trade paperback) 5 X8, 270 pp, $14.95.

206

Our books are guaranteed:

If a book has a defect, or doesn't hold up under normal use, or if you are unhappy in any way with one of our books, we are interested to know about it and will replace it and credit reasonable return shipping costs. Products with publisher defects (i.e., books with missing pages, etc.) may be returned at any time without authorization. However, we request that you describe the problem, to help us to continuously improve.

Books by Norman Mark

Lure of the Long-Legged Blond--Norman Mark (2005) A rollicking ride featuring a lovable, intellectually-challenged loser. An hysterical parody of detective tales for mature readers. ISBN 1-888725-57-5, 5 X 8, 212 pp $14.95

Order Form			
Item	Each	Quantity	Amount
Missouri (only) sales tax 6.325%			
Priority Shipping			$5.00
	Total		

Name:

Address:

BeachHouse Books
PO Box 7151
 Chesterfield, MO 63006-7151
(636) 394-4950
www.beachhousebooks.com